THE PENGUIN CLASSICS

FOUNDER EDITOR (1944–64): E. V. RIEU

MAXIM GORKY is the pen-name of Alexei Maximovich Peshkov, who was born in 1868 in the city of Nizhny-Novgorod, now renamed after him. After his father's death he spent his childhood with his mother and grandparents in an atmosphere of hostility. He was turned out of the house when his mother died and left to work in various jobs – in a bakery, in an ikon-maker's shop, on barges – until his unsuccessful attempt at suicide. For three years he wandered in the south like a tramp before publishing his first story, 'Makar Chudra', in a Tiflis newspaper. After his return to Nizhny he worked on another newspaper, in which many of his stories appeared; he quickly achieved fame and soon afterwards his play *The Lower Depths* was a triumphant success at the Moscow Arts Theatre. By now active in the revolutionary movement, he was arrested in 1905 by the Tsarist government but released following a petition signed by eminent statesmen and writers. While in America in 1906 he savagely attacked American capitalism, and wrote his best-selling novel, *Mother*. During the First World War he was associated with the Marxist Internationalist Group, and in 1917 he founded *New Life*, a daily devoted to left-wing socialism, but which outspokenly attacked Kerensky and Lenin's 'Communist hysteria'. In 1921 he went to Italy, where he wrote *My Universities*, the third part of his great autobiographical trilogy; the other parts are *My Childhood* and *My Apprenticeship*. He returned to Moscow in 1928, and from then on he was a champion of the Soviet cause. In 1936 he died – allegedly poisoned by his political enemies – and was given a hero's funeral in Red Square.

RONALD WILKS studied Russian language and literature at Trinity College, Cambridge. He has also translated 'The Little Demon' by Sologub, *Eugene Onegin* by Pushkin, *My Childhood* and *My Apprenticeship* by Gorky and Gogol's *Diary of a Madman*, published in the Penguin Classics.

MAXIM GORKY

MY UNIVERSITIES

TRANSLATED
WITH AN INTRODUCTION BY
RONALD WILKS

PENGUIN BOOKS

Penguin Books Ltd, Harmondsworth, Middlesex, England
Penguin Books, 625 Madison Avenue, New York, New York 10022, U.S.A.
Penguin Books Australia Ltd, Ringwood, Victoria, Australia
Penguin Books Canada Ltd, 2801 John Street, Markham, Ontario, Canada L3R 1B4
Penguin Books (N.Z.) Ltd, 182–190 Wairau Road, Auckland 10, New Zealand

—

This translation first published 1979

—

Copyright © Ronald Wilks, 1979
All rights reserved

—

Made and printed in Great Britain by
Richard Clay (The Chaucer Press) Ltd,
Bungay, Suffolk
Set in Monotype Garamond

Introduction

THE third part of Maxim Gorky's autobiographical trilogy was written in 1922 and published in the following year in the magazine *Red Virgin Soil*. Several major episodes in *My Universities* – the suicide attempt, life in Derenkov's bakery, are described in fuller detail in earlier stories such as *An Incident from the Life of Makar*, *The Boss*, and Gorky refers to both of these in the text of the present volume. The narrative of *My Universities* is continued in the later sketches and short stories *The Watchman*, *Days of Korolenko*, *First Love*. Gorky actually had intended publishing these and other sketches together with *My Universities*, in one volume, but he never carried this out.

In *My Apprenticeship* Gorky had portrayed his life in Nizhny-Novgorod with the Sergeyevs, describing the years from 1879 to 1884, when he left his native town for Kazan, with the intention of enrolling at the university there.

My Universities records Gorky's life up to 1888 (when he was twenty) and falls into two contrasting sections, the first describing his life in Kazan up to his attempted suicide in 1887, and the second his life in a small village thirty miles down the Volga. After a short while in the village he left for the South and eventually found work in a fishery on the shores of the Caspian.

Gorky tells us at the close of *My Apprenticeship*: 'I went to Kazan in the secret hope that I might somehow manage to enrol as a student there.' However, his hopes were dashed, as he was considered too young and ill-prepared. Since he was forced to try and earn a living for himself from a very early age, he had received no formal education whatsoever. He had managed to read a great deal and had shown a voracious appetite for all kinds of books – but only in the face of great difficulty: time and again he tells us he had to beg, borrow, and steal books, and we often see him poring over a book trying to read by a home-made candle, after a day of crippling work.

Therefore the irony of the title of the previous volume is continued, and Gorky's 'universities' were in actuality clandestine discussions with revolutionaries in dark cellars and secret meeting places, arguments with religious fanatics and highly eccentric schoolteachers – a truly harsh 'book of life'. Time for reading had to be fought for, with the constant threat of being discovered hanging over him. But he did manage to read a great deal, including socialist writers such as Chernyshevsky, Plekhanov and Lavrov.

The variety of people encountered by Gorky in *My Universities* is very striking, from the consumptive atheist Shaposhnikov, with his pathological hatred of God; theological students who hold orgies in brothels; the despicable Tolstoyan, Klopsky, who seduced two sisters; half-demented dreamers, aimless drifters, ardent revolutionaries. As in *My Apprenticeship* people are thrown about in life like flotsam, disappear, commit suicide, are arrested and sent to Siberia.

It was at this period in Gorky's life that he became involved with revolutionaries and the major part of *My Universities* is concerned with political activities, principally the Populist movement of the 1880s. Lenin, who was expelled from Kazan University during the disturbances of 1887, states that this part of the autobiographical trilogy was his favourite reading. Derenkov's bakery, where Gorky worked for a time, was a secret meeting place for young students and others who opposed the Tsarist government; later the bakery was characterized in a police report as an enterprise that had been 'established with suspicious aims'. It is possible that the loathsome policeman Nikiforych, who tries to make close friends with Gorky, and to make an informer out of him, was responsible for reporting the illegal activities there to the authorities. In a subsequent letter Gorky states that in reality he was far too busy working day and night (the

6

unremitting drudgery in that dark cellar of a bakery is wonderfully recorded in the famous story *Twenty six men and one girl*) for any revolutionary activities.

However, Gorky did try to incite his fellow workers to revolt against bad pay and conditions, but for the most part met with apathy. And Gorky repeatedly stresses his disenchantment with workers and peasants, and looked sadly on their drunkenness, apathy and inertia. For this reason he strongly criticizes books portraying the lives of workers as 'sweet and beautiful', and which delighted in singing the praises of the peasant with his simple wisdom: it was in this that Gorky showed himself sharply antagonistic to Tolstoy's idealization of the primitive virtue of the peasant.

Gorky refutes the abstract dogmas according to which the people were the 'incarnation of spiritual beauty and kindness' and writes: 'But I had never known any people who were really like this. I had seen carpenters, stevedores, bricklayers, men like Yakov, Osip, Grigory.' These men, whom he met in *My Apprenticeship*, and later, were a source of sad disillusion, and books describing their virtues and spiritual beauty were nothing but fiction. These men were never 'God-like, the repository of all that was beautiful, just and majestic'.

The workmen in that dark sooty bakery cellar were totally unresponsive to his exhortations to seek a better life and considered him an 'amusing clown'. Later in *My Universities*, when Gorky joins Romas to help him start a fruit-growing collective to protect the peasants against the *kulak* farmers he finds the same total lack of response. And when the shop is finally burned down by peasants for selling goods too cheaply Gorky decides he has had enough and leaves for the Caspian. In his depiction of his life at Krasnovidovo, in the latter part of *My Universities*, Gorky provides a stark picture of the decomposition of the Russian village in the face of the growing tide of capitalism.

In this last part of his autobiographical trilogy Gorky submits himself to relentless self-analysis – much more so

7

than in the earlier volumes. Books, he tells us, really provided no answer to his searchings, and he states that he 'seldom found ideas in books which I had not already encountered in reality.' And his bewilderment in the face of the many and varied 'philosophies' offered him by the students and teachers with whom he mixed confused him even more. Clearly he saw himself as a host of contradictions, and felt that he was being 'drawn in all directions'. The hard world, as in his life before, conflicted sharply with what his reading had led him to expect and he concluded that he would always be a misfit and never find his true place in life. With the typical self-criticism of an adolescent, lacking all confidence and very unsure of himself, he tells us: 'On the whole, I did not care for myself . . . I thought of myself as clumsy and coarse. I disliked my face with its high Kalmyk cheek-bones, and my voice, which did not obey me.' Besides intellectual, there were sexual problems and he is mocked by his fellow workers for his extreme timidity and priggishness. All of these factors, combined with the forces of crippling drudgery that had been undermining his strength for some considerable time, led to a complete breakdown and his attempt at suicide.

This took place in the December of 1887, when he bought a revolver and tried to shoot himself through the heart. The bullet missed, but caused permanent damage to his lungs. In a local newspaper his suicide note was recorded: 'I ask you to blame the German poet Heine for my death, he invented toothache in the heart. I ask you to dissect my heart to see what kind of devil was in me.' Gorky was dismissed from hospital after ten days, but the matter did not end there, and the suicide note eventually came into the hands of the Kazan ecclesiastical authorities, who excommunicated Gorky for seven years, which certainly did not cause him any concern.

It was Romas, the worldly peasant who had just returned from a prison term in Siberia, who 'saved' him. The practical wisdom of this simple peasant is strongly contrasted with the half-baked 'philosophies' and empty theorizing he had encountered in both books and people. Romas helped Gorky recover his self-respect, advising him to study and never once embarrassing him by asking the reasons for the suicide attempt.

After three years of wandering in the South, Gorky finally went to Tiflis, where in 1892 the editor of the newspaper the *Caucasus,* impressed with the way he told of his adventures (in this most eventful of lives) made him sit down in his office and write them down. The result was his first published story *Makar Chudra,* signed with the pen-name M. Gorky. In the following year with the help of Lanin and Korolenko, he obtained a post on a local paper. Thus began his literary career.

R.W.

TO GISELA

Translator

My Universities

AND SO I went to study in no less a place than the University of Kazan. A student called N. Yevreinov, a likeable handsome young man with the tender eyes of a woman, first gave me the idea. He lived in the same house as me, up in the attic, and became very interested in me, seeing how often I had a book in my hand. We introduced ourselves, and before long Yevreinov was trying to convince me that I possessed 'an exceptional talent for learning'. 'You were fashioned by nature to serve learning,' he would say, and he looked very handsome when he shook his mane of long hair.

At that time I was completely ignorant of the fact that one could serve scholarship like a rabbit, and as Yevreinov demonstrated so clearly, what universities needed was young men, just like myself. And, of course, the ghost of the illustrious Mikhail Lomonosov* was invoked. Yevreinov said that I would live with him in Kazan, spend the autumn and winter studying at the Gymnasium and then, after passing 'some kind of' examination (he often used this phrase) I would receive a government grant from the University and earn the title of 'scholar' after five years. It all sounded so simple, because Yevreinov was nineteen and he had a good heart.

When he had passed his exams he left and two weeks later I followed him. As she said good-bye Grandmother gave me the following advice: 'Now, don't get angry with people, you're in the habit of doing that the whole time and you've become bossy and arrogant. It all comes from your Grandfather. But what is he, after all? He's lived his life and he's turned out a fool, a bitter old man. Now don't you forget that God doesn't judge people – that would be too flattering for the Devil! Well, good-bye now . . .' As she wiped the meagre tears from her swarthy, flabby cheeks, she added: 'We shan't see each

* First great Russian scientist and linguist (1711–65). (Trans.)

other ever again. You're a rolling stone and now you're going a long way away, and I'll soon be dead . . .'

For some time now I had drifted away from that dear old woman and I rarely saw her. And now came the painful, sudden realization that I would never meet anyone so close to me again, someone who would be so much a part of me.

I stood at the stern of the ship and saw her standing there on the quayside, crossing herself with one hand while with the other she wiped her face with the corner of her old shawl – that face with dark eyes shining with an undying love of people.

And here I was in a half Tartar city, in a little room in a single-storeyed house which stood by itself on a small hill at the end of a narrow, miserable street. One of the walls overlooked a piece of waste ground where once there had been a fire. It was overgrown with weeds. The ruins of the brick building that had once stood there stuck out among the thickets of wormwood, burdock, horse sorrel and broom, and underneath was a large cellar in which stray dogs lived and died. I remember that cellar very well – it became one of my universities.

The Yevreinovs (the mother and her two sons) tried to make ends meet on a wretched pension. From my very first days there I saw how that little grey widow, with a sadness that was so tragic to watch, used to come back from the market, lay out her shopping on the kitchen table and then try to solve the difficult problem of making a decent meal for three healthy young men from a few scraps of tough meat, without even thinking of herself. She never said very much and her grey eyes were hardened with the hopeless, ineffectual obstinacy of an old horse that, having exhausted all its strength, still tries to drag its load up a hill, and knowing very well that it won't make the top, carries on all the same.

One morning, about three days after I arrived, when the two sons were still asleep in the kitchen and I was helping the mother to clean some vegetables, she asked me in a gentle, cautious voice: 'Why did you come here?'

14

'To study at the university.'

As she spoke her eyebrows moved upwards together with the yellow, leathery skin of her forehead. The knife slipped and she cut her finger badly. She sank back onto a chair as she sucked the blood from the wound, but immediately jumped to her feet again and said: 'Oh, hell!'

She bandaged her finger with her handkerchief and praised me.

'You're very good at peeling potatoes.'

It would have been very surprising if I wasn't! I told her about my work on the steamboat and she asked: 'Do you think *that* qualifies you for entering the university?'

At that period in my life my sense of humour was not very keen. I took her question seriously and told her about my intended course of action, as a result of which the doors of that temple of learning would open up for me. She sighed and said: 'Oh, Nikolai, Nikolai!'

At that moment Nikolai came into the kitchen for a wash – he was heavy with sleep, his hair dishevelled. He looked as cheerful as ever.

'Mama, some meat dumplings would be a good idea!'

'Yes, a good idea,' she agreed.

As I wanted to show off my knowledge of the art of cooking I told her that the meat was not good enough for making dumplings. Anyway, there was not enough.

This infuriated Varvara Ivanovna and she directed some expressions at me that were so strong they made my ears burn and turn upwards. She threw a bundle of carrots on the table and left the kitchen. Nikolai winked at me and explained her behaviour: 'She's feeling a bit low today.'

He settled down on a bench and informed me that, on the whole, women tended to be more highly strung than men – that was part of their nature – and that this had been proved beyond all shadow of doubt by a very learned Swiss scholar. An Englishman called John Stuart Mill had said something on the subject as well. Nikolai loved lecturing me and he took advantage of every opportunity for stuffing my brain with something that was 'absolutely necessary' and without which it was 'impossible to live'. I would listen to him eagerly and in a very short time Foucault, La Rochefoucauld and La Rochejaquelin all merged into one and the same person. I could not remember whose head was cut off by whom, if Lavoisier had beheaded Dumouriez, or if it was the other way round. That fine young man sincerely wished to 'make a man out of me' and he confidently promised to accomplish this. But in actual fact, he did not have the time, nor was he in a position where he could take me seriously in hand. His youthful egoism and irresponsibility blinded him, so that he just could not see how cunning and hard-working his mother had to be in order to run the household. His younger brother, a rather dull-witted, taciturn student at the gymnasium, was even less aware of this. But for a long time now I had come to know, in all their finer points, the complicated conjuring tricks which the chemistry and economics of cooking involved and I clearly saw the sheer cunning of that woman, who was forced every single day to deceive her sons' stomachs and feed such an unpleasant-looking, badly-mannered vagrant.

Naturally, every slice of bread that was shared out to me lay like a heavy stone on my conscience.

So I went out to look for a job, whatever it might be. I would leave the house first thing in the morning to avoid eating there. If the weather was bad I would spend the time sitting in the cellar on the waste ground. As I sat there among the stinking carcases of dogs and cats, listening to the pouring rain and sighing wind, I soon came to realize that the university was a wild dream and I would have done better to stick to my original intention of running away to Persia. Already I pictured myself as a grey-bearded wizard with a magic formula for producing grain the size of apples, potatoes weighing nearly forty pounds each and, in general, as someone bringing many blessings into a world where life was so diabolical – and not only for myself. I had already learned how to dream of strange adventures and heroic deeds. This was of great help to me on those days when life was particularly hard – and since

16

there were plenty of these I became an accomplished dreamer. I did not expect help from anyone around me, or hope that I might have a sudden stroke of luck: but I was gradually developing great strength of will and persistence in whatever I did.

The harder life became, the stronger and wiser I felt. I understood at a very early age that men are created by their resilience to their environment. To ward off starvation I used to go down to the wharves along the Volga, where it was easy to earn fifteen or twenty kopecks. Surrounded by stevedores, tramps and thieves, I felt just like a piece of iron thrown onto a heap of red-hot coal, and every day filled me with countless impressions that were painful and not easily forgotten. Those men there, with their naked greed and crude instincts spun before me like a whirlwind, and their angry feelings towards life, their derisively hostile attitude towards the whole world, their indifference to what happened to themselves, appealed to me. All that I had directly experienced in my own life drew me towards them and made me want to plunge myself into that same cynical world.

Bret Harte and the huge quantity of cheap novels I had read only made me sympathize with them all the more.

The consumptive Bashkin, a man who had been cruelly beaten in his time, who was once a student at a teacher's training college and who had now turned professional thief, used to give me eloquent little sermons: 'Why are you so shy, just like a young girl? Afraid of losing your honour? That's all a virgin has to lose, but for you it's a millstone round your neck. An ox is honest, so all it gets is hay.'

He had reddish hair, was clean shaven, like an actor, and the nimble, gentle movements of his small body reminded me of a kitten. He behaved towards me like a teacher, wanting to take me under his wing and I felt that he sincerely wanted me to be successful and happy. Bashkin was very clever, and he had read many good books – the *Count of Monte Cristo* was his favourite.

'That book has a purpose *and* a heart,' he would say.

17

He liked women and talked about them rapturously, smacking his lips in relish as his broken body twitched convulsively. There was something morbid about these jerks of his and they repelled me. But I listened to what he said attentively, appreciating the beauty of his words.

'Oh, women, women!' he would say in a sing-song voice and the blood would rush to his sallow face and his dark eyes gleamed with delight. 'I would go through anything for a woman. Like the devil, they don't know sin! Stay in love – no one's ever thought of anything better.'

He was a talented story-teller and effortlessly composed little songs for the prostitutes about the sorrows of unhappy love. These songs of his were sung in all the towns along the Volga. He was the author of that very popular song:

> 'I'm a poor girl, and no beauty,
> And I'm very badly dressed,
> Who would ever want to marry,
> A poor girl like me . . .?'

Trusov, a mysterious, good-looking character who dressed rather flashily and who had the thin fingers of a musician, was very kind to me. He owned a shop in the Admiralty quarter and although his board bore the sign 'Watchmaker', he actually lived by selling stolen goods.

'Peshkov! Don't you ever teach yourself thieves' tricks!' he would say, solemnly stroking his grey beard and screwing up his cunning, bold eyes. 'I can see that you're cut out to be something else, you're a *spiritual* person.'

'What do you mean *spiritual*?'

'I mean someone without any trace of jealousy in him, only curiosity . . .'

As far as I was concerned this was far from the truth, since I was very jealous of a lot of things. Moreover, Bashkin's ability to express himself in a peculiar, almost poetical style, with unexpected similes and turns of phrase, made me envious. I remember the beginning of one of his stories about a love affair. 'One dull night I was sitting in my room, like an owl in the hollow of a tree, in the poor little town of Sviyazhsk. It was autumn, October, and outside the lazy little rain was falling. I could hear the wind breathing like an angry Tartar singing his endless songs: O-o-o-u-u-u. And then she came, light and rosy as a cloud at sunrise, but her eyes shone with a deceptive purity of soul. "My dear," she said in that honest-sounding voice, "I've not been unfaithful." I knew that she was lying, but all the same I believed it was the truth! Reason firmly told me it wasn't so, but in my heart I just couldn't believe it.' As he spoke he swayed rhythmically to and fro, covering his eyes and gently touching himself over the heart. His voice was dull and lifeless, but his words were bright and clear, like a nightingale's song.

I was jealous of Trusov. Here was a man who spoke so fascinatingly about Siberia, Khiva and Bokhara, so comically and maliciously about bishops. Once he said something about Alexander III in a mysterious voice: 'That Tsar knows his job all right!'

Trusov struck me as one of those 'villains' who at the end of a novel, much to the reader's surprise, turn into magnanimous heroes.

Sometimes, on stifling nights, men would cross the river Kazanka to the meadows, and lie among the bushes, drinking, eating, chatting about their personal affairs, but more often about the complexities of life, about the strange muddle of human relationships. But mostly they would discuss women. They talked about them with bitterness and with sorrow, sometimes very touchingly and almost always with strong feelings, as though they were peering into a dark place filled with painful surprises. I spent about three weeks with them under that dark sky with its dim stars, down in the stifling heat of a hollow thickly overgrown with willows. On those dark nights, when one could sense from the dampness in the air that the Volga was near, the lights of masts on the ships seemed to be crawling everywhere, like golden spiders, and the dark mass of the hilly bank was dotted with little fiery patches and veins of light – these were windows in pubs and houses in the prosperous village of Uslon. The blades of paddle wheels made a dull sound as they threshed the water and it broke one's heart to hear those men howling like wolves as they stood on trains of barges. Somewhere I could hear a hammer striking iron and a mournful song drifting over the water, as though someone's soul were gently smouldering, bringing a sadness that lay on one's heart like ashes.

And it was even sadder listening to the softly flowing words of the men meditating on life, each speaking about what interested him alone and hardly paying any attention to what the others said. As they sat down or sprawled out under the bushes they smoked cigarettes and now and again, without any sign of greediness, would sip just a little vodka or beer and then let themselves drift backwards into the past, along the path of memories.

One of them who seemed flattened against the earth by the pitch-black night said: 'Listen to what happened to me once . . .'

'Things like that happen . . . all the time . . .' the others would agree after hearing the story.

All I could hear was the words 'happened', 'happens', 'used to happen' and it seemed to me that during the course of that night the men had reached the last hours of their life: everything was past and done with, nothing would ever happen again!

It was feelings such as these that alienated me from Bashkin and Trusov, but I liked them all the same. And if I tried to think really logically about all that I had been through, then it would have been only natural for me to have gone off with them. My outraged hopes of bettering myself, of becoming a student also drew me towards them. In times of hunger, anger and weariness I felt quite capable of committing any crime, and not only against the 'sacred institution of private property'. However, the romantic urges of youth prevented me leaving the path that I was destined to tread. By this time, besides the humane stories of Bret Harte and various cheap novels, I had read quite a few serious books that aroused a yearning for something that was still very vague, but which I knew had more meaning than anything I saw around me. And at the same time I made new friends, and new impressions were born. The boys from the gymnasium used to go and play skittles on the waste ground next to the Yevreinovs and one of them, Gury Pletnyov, enchanted me.

He had a dark skin, the blue-black hair of a Japanese, and his face was covered with tiny black spots, just as though someone had rubbed it all over with gunpowder. He was irrepressibly cheerful, good at games, a witty conversationalist, and endowed with many different talents that were still in embryo. Like all talented Russians he was content to live simply on what nature had given him and he made no effort at all to cultivate or develop it. He had a keen ear and a marvellous feeling for music, which he loved. He could play the *gusli**, balalaika, and accordion extremely well, but he made no effort at all to master more refined or difficult instruments. He was poor and badly dressed, but his torn and crumpled shirt, his patched trousers, and his worn-out shoes that were full of holes, seemed to harmonize perfectly with his swaggering manner, the lively movements of his body and sweeping gestures.

He was like a man who had just got up after a long and painful illness, or a prisoner who had just been freed. Everything in life was new for him, pleasant; everything sent him into fits of boisterous gaiety and he jumped around like a fire-cracker.

When he discovered how painful and dangerous my life was he invited me to live with him and study to be a teacher in a village school. And so I found myself in a strange, but very cheerful, tenement called the Marusovka – familiar in all probability to many a generation of Kazan students. It was a large, dilapidated house on Rybnoryadsky Street and appeared to

* gusli – a kind of psaltery (trans.)

have been captured from its owners by the hungry students, prostitutes, and living phantoms of people who had outlived their time.

Pletnyov's room was in the space under the stairs leading up to the attic. His entire furniture consisted of a camp-bed and a table and chair by the window at the end of the corridor. There were three doors in this passage and behind two of them lived prostitutes. Behind the third was a consumptive maths teacher from a church school, a tall, scraggy, almost terrifying man who seemed to have coarse reddish wool growing everywhere and whose filthy old rags barely covered him – his shiny blue skin and skeletal ribs showed through the holes in the most ghastly way.

It seemed that his only food was his own finger nails, which he had gnawed until they bled. Day and night he sat there making drawings and calculations, and he coughed incessantly, making hollow, booming sounds. The prostitutes were afraid of him and thought that he was mad. But they felt sorry for him and used to put bread, tea or sugar outside his door, in little packets. He would pick these up and carry them away, wheezing like a tired old horse. If they forgot to leave anything for some reason or other, or were unable to, he would open his door and shout down the corridor in his rasping voice: 'Give me some bread!'

The pride of a maniac happy in the knowledge of his own greatness gleamed in the dark pits of his deep sunken eyes. Now and again he was visited by a hunchbacked little grey-haired freak of a man with a twisted leg who wore very strong glasses over his puffy nose, and whose craftily smiling sallow face put one in mind of a castrate. Both of them would make sure the door was tightly shut and sit for hours on end in mysterious silence. Once, however, quite late at night, I was woken up by the mathematician screaming in a hoarse, violent voice: 'But I'm telling you that it's a prison! Geometry's a cage, yes! A mousetrap! A prison!' The hunchback freak squealed with laughter and kept on repeating some incomprehensible words. Then the mathematician suddenly bellowed: 'To hell with you, clear off!' When his guest had rolled out into the corridor, hissing, squealing and wrapping himself up in his broad cloak, the mathematician stood at the door, a tall and terrifying figure. He ran his fingers through his dishevelled hair and said in a wheezing voice: 'Euclid is an idiot! An id-i-ot! I can prove that God has more brains than that Greek!' And he slammed the door so hard that something in his room crashed to the floor.

I soon discovered that this man was trying to prove God's existence by mathematics. But he died before he could do this.

Pletnyov worked as a proof-reader on the night shift at a newspaper office, for which he earned himself eleven kopecks. If I happened to come back without any money we had to live on four pounds of bread, two kopecks' worth of tea and three kopecks' worth of sugar a day. I never really had the time to go out and earn anything, since I had to stick to my studies. This I found extremely difficult. Grammar, with all its ugly, narrow rules and ossified formulae, was particularly depressing and I was quite hopeless at squeezing into them a language so alive and so difficult, so capriciously flexible as Russian. But before long, much to my pleasure, I discovered that I had started 'too early' and that, even if I did manage to pass exams that would have qualified me to teach in the village schools, I would not have been accepted on account of my age.

I shared the same bunk as Pletnyov: I slept in it at night, when he was at work, and he used it during the day. He would return early in the morning, exhausted from lack of sleep, his face even swarthier and his eyes inflamed. I would immediately go out to the pub and get some hot water – it goes without saying that we could not afford a samovar. Then we would sit by the window with our tea and bread. Gury used to tell me all the latest news from the newspaper office and recite amusing verses written by an alcoholic columnist who went under the name of 'Red Domino'. His light-hearted attitude to life amused me and it seemed just like that of the fat-faced

Galkina, who sold women's second-hand clothes in the market and who was a procuress. This was the woman from whom Gury rented his little corner under the stairs. As he never had any money to pay the rent he would entertain her with jokes, by playing the accordion and singing sentimental songs instead. A smile gleamed in his eyes when he sang in his slight tenor voice.

When she was a girl Galkina had performed at the opera and she knew all about singing. Often floods of tiny tears would roll down from that woman's cheeky eyes onto her puffy bluish glutton and drunkard's cheeks, and she would brush them away with her flabby fingers, carefully drying them with her filthy handkerchief.

'Oh, Gurochka!' she would sigh, 'you're an *artist*! If only you were a little more handsome I could fix you up all right! I've lost count of all the *youthies* like you I've fixed up with women because they got miserable on their own!'

One of these 'youthies' lived right over us. He was a student and the son of a furrier's assistant. He was of average height and broad in the chest. His terribly narrow hips made him look like a triangle standing on its apex which had been slightly broken off at the tip. The soles of his feet were small, just like a woman's. He had a small head that was deeply sunk between the shoulders, and he had reddish, bristly hair. His great pale green eyes looked out gloomily from his white anaemic face.

After great efforts on his part – he often went hungry, like a stray dog – and much against his father's wishes, he managed to finish his course at the gymnasium and get a place at the University. But he then discovered that he had a smooth bass voice, so he decided to take up singing instead. Galkina soon settled him with a rich merchant's wife about forty years old, with one son already in his third year and a daughter who had just left the gymnasium. She was a scraggy-looking woman, flat-chested and stiff as a soldier, and with the dried-up face of an ascetic nun. Her large grey eyes were hidden in their dark sockets. She always wore black, with an old-fashioned silk scarf over her head. Earrings made from some sort of poisonous-looking green stone shook when she moved her ears.

Sometimes during the evening or early morning she would visit her student, and more than once I saw her almost leaping through the front gates and striding with determination across the yard. Her face was quite frightening, and she pressed her lips so tightly they almost completely disappeared. Her eyes had a wide-open look and gazed wearily and hopelessly straight ahead. But to me she appeared to be blind. She was not really ugly, but nervous stress had disfigured her, stiffened her body and given her face a horribly pinched look.

'Watch out!' Pletnyov used to say. 'I think she's mad.'

The student hated her and avoided her as much as he could. But she pursued him, just like a spy or some ruthless creditor.

After he had had a few drinks he would confess: 'I'm quite bewildered by all this! What do I want with singing? With my ugly mug and a figure like mine they wouldn't even let me on to the stage, oh no!'

'Why don't you finish with her?' Pletnyov advised him.

'Yes, you're right. But I'm sorry for her. I can't stand the sight of her, yet I'm sorry . . . If only you *knew* how she . . . oh . . .'

We already knew, since we had heard how that woman would stand on the stairs at night pleading with him in her empty, trembling voice: 'For Christ's sake, dear, please!'

She owned a large factory, houses, horses, donated thousands of roubles to a midwives' training school. But she pleaded for love, just like a beggar asking for charity.

After tea Pletnyov would go to bed while I went out to try and find some work and I came back in the evening just when Gury was going off to the printing office. If I managed to bring back some food – bread, sausage or boiled tripe – we would share everything equally and he would take his portion off to work. When he had left I used to wander down the corridors and passages in the Marusovka, taking a close look at the lives of all those people who were so new and unfamiliar. The house was swarming with them, just like an ant-hill. It was full of acrid, sour smells and thick, hostile shadows lurked in every corner. The noise went on from morning until late at night – the incessant hum of seamstresses' sewing machines, chorus girls from the operetta practising their voices, the cooing sound of the student with his deep voice going up and down the scales, the loud exclamations of the half-demented actor who had taken to drink, the hysterical bawling of tipsy prostitutes: I was faced with a natural, but insoluble question: 'What is it all for?'

A red-haired, bald man with high cheek-bones, a large stomach, thin legs, a huge mouth and horsey teeth which earned him the nickname of 'Chestnut' used aimlessly to hang around these hungry young people. He was in the third year of a lawsuit with some relatives, who were merchants from Simbirsk and he used to tell each and every one of us: 'I don't want to go on living any more, but before I die I'll *ruin* them! Then they'll wander around like beggars and have to live on charity for three years, and afterwards I'll return everything I'm suing them for – I'll give it all back and ask them: "Well, you devils? What have you got to say now?"'

'Is that your aim in life, Chestnut?' they would ask.

'Yes, that's what I've set my whole heart on, and there's nothing else I want.'

For days on end he would hang around the local courts, the High Court, and call on his lawyer. Often in the evening he would come back in a cab with a whole pile of bags, parcels, bottles and give wild parties in his filthy room with its sagging ceiling and uneven floor. He invited the students and seamstresses – everyone, in fact, who wanted to stuff himself with food and have a few drinks. 'Chestnut' would only drink rum, which had left indelible dark reddish stains on the table-cloth, his clothes, and even on the floor. When he had drunk a few glasses he would start wailing: 'You're my dear little birds! I love you, you're all honest people. But I'm a rotten devil and a cr-cro-codile! All I want is to ruin my relatives and I'll do it! God, I don't want to live any more!' Chestnut's eyes would blink gloomily and drunken tears would wash that stupid face with its high cheek-bones. He would wipe them away with the palm of his hand and then rub it on his knees. His trousers were always covered with greasy stains.

'And how do *you* manage to live?' he would shout. 'Cold and hunger, rotten clothes. Is it all decreed by some law? What can you hope to learn with that kind of a life? Oh, if only the Tsar knew what lives you lead . . .' Then he would pull a handful of different coloured banknotes from his pocket and ask: 'Well, who wants some money? Take it, my dear friends!' The chorus girls and seamstresses would greedily snatch the money out of his hairy hand and this made him laugh out loud and say: 'That's not for you, it's for the students.'

But the students would not take the money. The furrier's son shouted angrily: 'To hell with the money!' On one occasion, when he was drunk, he brought Pletnyov a bundle of ten-rouble notes crumpled up into a ball. He threw them onto the table and said: 'Well, do *you* need them? I don't.' Then he lay down on our bunk and started howling and sobbing so much that we had to give him a drink and pour cold water over him. When he had fallen asleep Pletnyov tried to smooth out the crumpled bank-notes, but it was impossible: they were so tightly rolled that we had to separate them by moistening. It was stifling, cramped, noisy and nightmarish in that dirty, smoky room with its windows facing the stone wall of the house next door.

Chestnut roared louder than anyone. I asked him: 'Why do you live here and not in a hotel?'

'My dear friend . . . it's for my *soul*! Being here with you warms it up . . .'

The furrier's son confirmed this: 'That's true, Chestnut! I feel the same. If I lived anywhere else I'd be finished.'

Chestnut would ask Pletnyov: 'Play us a tune, give us a song.'

Gury would put his *gusli* on his knees and start singing: 'Rise, rise oh beautiful sun . . .' His soft voice went straight to one's heart.

The whole room fell quiet and everyone sat deep in thought listening to those plaintive words and the quiet strumming of the *gusli*.

'Hell, that sounds good!' muttered that unhappy comforter of merchant women. Gury Pletnyov who was endowed with that brand of wisdom called cheerfulness played the good fairy among the strange inhabitants of that house. His soul, which seemed to have been dyed in the bright colours of youth, brightened those dark lives with the fireworks of wonderful jokes, good songs, witty ridicule of people's morals and habits, and outspoken comments on the gross injustice of life.

He was only just twenty, and looked like a mere boy. But everyone in that house treated him as someone they could rely upon for good advice in difficult times and who was always ready to help in one way or another. The better people there loved him and the nasty ones were afraid of him. Even old Nikiforych the policeman always greeted him with his foxy smile.

The yard of the Marusovka was used as a general thoroughfare and as it sloped away uphill it joined two streets, Rybnoryadsky with Staro-Gorshechny, on one corner of which Nikiforych's sentry box cosily snuggled not far away from the gates of our house. Nikiforych was the senior policeman in our neighbourhood and he was a tall, lean man whose chest was covered with medals. He had a clever face, a friendly smile, and cunning eyes.

He was very interested in our noisy colony, which consisted of people of the past and of the future. Several times a day his neatly-built figure made its appearance in the yard and he never hurried as he paced up and down, peering into every window like a zoo-keeper doing his rounds of the cages.

One winter a one-armed officer by the name of Smirnov

and a soldier called Muratov were arrested – both of them had been awarded the Cross of Georgia and had served under Skobelyev in the Akhal-Tekin Expedition. Together with five others – Zobnin, Ovsyankin, Grigoryev, Krylov and someone else – they were arrested for attempting to set up a secret printing press. One Sunday, in broad daylight, Muratov and Smirnov tried to steal some type face from Klyuchnikov's press, which was situated in one of the busiest streets, and there they were caught. And one night the gendarmes arrested a tall gloomy man in the Marusovka whom I had nicknamed 'Wandering Belfry'. When Gury heard about this next morning he rumpled his thick black hair excitedly and said: 'Run over there, as quick as hell, Maksimych . . .'

After explaining where I should run he added: 'But be very careful, there might be detectives.'

I was delighted at this mysterious mission and flew as swift as a martin to the Admiralty suburb. When I reached the coppersmith's dark workshop I could make out the figure of a young man with curly hair and remarkably blue eyes. He was plating a saucepan, but he did not look like a workman at all. In one corner a little old man with a small strap round his hair was grinding a tap in a vice.

I asked the coppersmith: 'Any work?'

The old man answered angrily: 'We've got work, but there's none for you!' The young man gave me a quick glance and then leaned over the saucepan again. I gently nudged his leg with mine, and he furiously stared at me in amazement with those blue eyes, holding the saucepan by the handle as though he were about to hurl it at me. But as soon as he saw me wink he calmly said: 'Well get out of here, get out.'

I winked at him once again and went out into the street. The curly-haired boy stretched himself and followed, silently staring at me as he smoked a cigarette.

'Are you Tikhon?' I asked.

'Yes.'

'Pyotr's been arrested.'

He frowned angrily and seemed to be testing me with his eyes.

'Which Pyotr?'

'The tall one, like a deacon.'

'Anything else?'

'Nothing.'

'What do *I* want with this Pyotr and deacons and all the rest of them?' the coppersmith asked and the way he asked this finally convinced me that he was not a workman. I ran home and was very proud that I had fulfilled my mission. This was the first time I had taken part in 'conspiratorial' activities.

Gury Pletnyov was closely connected with them, but when I asked to be allowed to join the circle he said: 'It's too early for that, my friend! You keep on with your studies.'

Yevreinov introduced me to a very mysterious man. This introduction was ringed around with such precautions that I felt something very important was in the air. Yevreinov took me beyond the city, to the Arsky Field, and on the way he warned that I should have to be extremely careful as far as this new acquaintance was concerned and keep the whole thing a complete secret. Then he pointed out a little grey figure in the distance slowly making its way across the deserted field. Yevreinov first looked round and then said softly: 'That's him! Follow him, and when he stops, go up and say: "I'm just passing by."'

I had always found mysterious things pleasant, but now it all seemed too absurd on that scorching, bright day, with that solitary figure swaying like a greyish blade of grass in the fields, and nothing more. I caught up with him by the cemetery gates and saw that he was a young man with a small, dried-up looking face and forbidding eyes that were round as a bird's. He was dressed in a student's grey overcoat, but its shiny buttons had been ripped off and replaced by black ones made of bone. On his worn-out cap was a patch where a crest had once been. He seemed like a prematurely plucked bird and seemed to be in a hurry to prove to himself that he was already mature.

We sat down among the graves in the shade of some thick bushes. He had a cold business-like voice and I took a dislike to everything about him. When he had stiffly cross-examined me as to what I had read, he invited me to join a small circle that he had organized. I accepted and we parted. He went first, cautiously looking round the empty field.

I was the youngest in that circle, which was made up of another three or four young men, and I was quite unprepared for studying the works of John Stuart Mill, with Chernyshevsky's commentary. We used to meet in a flat belonging to a student called Milovsky from the teachers' training school and he later wrote stories under the pseudonym of Yeleonsky. After he had written about five volumes he committed suicide – so many people I knew made voluntary exits from life!

He was rather a quiet man, with a cautious mind, and careful in his choice of words. He lived in the cellar of a filthy house and worked as a joiner just for 'equilibrium of body and soul'. He was boring company. I did not find John Stuart Mill very fascinating and soon realized that I was very well acquainted with the basic principles of economics – I had learned them from direct experience of life and they were engraved on my skin. And it struck me that it was a waste of time writing books filled with difficult phrases about things that should have been clear to anyone who toiled for the well-being and comfort of 'others'. It called for a great effort to sit two or three hours in that dark pit which was heavy with the smell of glue, watching the wood-lice crawling up and down the filthy walls.

Once our preceptor failed to turn up at the usual time. We thought that he was not coming at all so we arranged a little party and bought a bottle of vodka, some bread and some cucumbers. Suddenly we glimpsed the grey legs of our teacher flashing past the window up above. We just had time to hide the vodka under the table before he came into the room and started elucidating Chernyshevsky's clever deductions. We all sat there still as statues, terrified that one of us might knock the bottle over with his foot. But the instructor himself knocked it over. He peered under the table and did not say one word. We would have felt better if he had sworn at us instead! His long silence, his stern face with its screwed up, hurt-looking eyes embarrassed me terribly. When I looked out of the corner of my eye at my friends' faces that had turned purple with shame I felt like a criminal and I was deeply sorry for him, although buying the vodka had not been my idea. It was boring at those readings and I wanted to go off instead to the Tartar quarter, where good-hearted, friendly people lived their own pure and clean lives. They spoke a very funny kind of broken Russian. In the evenings I could hear the strange voices of the muezzins calling from the high minarets and I thought that their lives were ordered in a way different from mine, that they were strange, quite unlike anything I knew and this brought me little joy.

The music of toiling men drew me down to the Volga. Even now it has an intoxicating effect and I remember very clearly that day when I first became aware of the heroic poetry of everyday life.

A great barge laden with goods from Persia ran aground on a rock below Kazan and smashed its bottom in. A gang of stevedores took me on to help unload the cargo. It was September, the wind was blowing upstream and made the waves angrily dance on the grey river as it savagely tore at their crests, whipping up a cold spray. The fifty men who made up the gang gloomily huddled under tarpaulins and old mats on the deck of an empty barge that a little tug had in tow, panting away as it scattered red sheaves of sparks into the driving rain.

Evening drew on. That leaden, watery sky sank low over the river and grew dark. The men swore and grumbled at the rain, at the wind, and at life as they lazily crawled round the deck trying to shelter from the cold and the wet. I thought that these men, who seemed to be half asleep, were incapable of any work and could never save that sinking cargo. Towards midnight we reached the shoals and moored our empty barge alongside the wreck. The foreman, a pock-faced, venomous, cunning old man with a filthy tongue and the eyes and nose of a kite, pulled his soaked cap off his bald head and shouted in the shrill voice of a woman: 'Time for prayers, lads!'

The stevedores bunched together into a black mass on the dark deck and growled like bears. The foreman finished his prayers first and screeched: 'Get some lamps! Come on, let's have some work out of you! Come on, lads, God help us!'

And those ponderous lazy men, drenched by the rain, began to show how they could work. Just as though they were going into battle they rushed onto the deck and down into the holds of the grounded barge, whooping, roaring and cracking jokes. Sacks of rice, boxes of raisins, hides, furs from Astrakhan, flew past me like feather cushions. Stocky figures tore by, urging each other on with their howling, whistling and violent swearing. It was hard to believe that these were the same morose, sluggish men who only a few minutes before had been gloomily complaining about life, rain and the cold – now they were working away gaily and quickly, and with great skill. The rain became heavier and colder, the wind rose and tugged at their shirts, blowing them up over their heads and baring their stomachs. In that damp murkiness, dark figures worked by the dim light of six lamps and their feet made a dull, thudding sound on the decks. They worked as though they had been starved of it and as though they had been waiting a long time for the sheer pleasure of throwing sacks weighing 160 pounds or more to each other, and tearing around with bales on their backs. And they worked as though they were playing a game, with all the gay enthusiasm of children, with that drunken joy of activity only surpassed in sweetness by a woman's embraces.

A huge bearded man, wet and slippery from the rain, in a tight fitting coat – clearly the owner of the cargo or his agent –

suddenly roared words of encouragement: 'Three gallons of vodka for you! No, you thieves, I'll make it six! Come on!'

Deep voices bellowed back at him through the darkness from every side: 'Make it nine!'

'Done! But finish the job first!'

And the whirlwind of work gathered impetus.

I joined in, grabbed some sacks, dragged them down and threw them to someone. Then I ran back for more and it seemed that I too was caught up with everything and whirling around in a mad dance. Those men could go on working furiously and gaily without getting tired, without sparing themselves, for months, for years, and they would have no trouble in seizing belfries and minarets in the town and taking them wherever they wanted to!

I spent that night in a state of ecstasy that I had never experienced before. My soul was brightened by the desire to spend my whole life in that half-insane rapture of work. Waves danced around the sides of the barges, rain lashed the decks, and the wind whistled over the river. In the greyish haze of the dawn half-wet naked figures ran swiftly and incessantly, shouting, laughing and revelling in their own strength and labour.

And suddenly the wind tore apart that heavy mass of clouds and a pinkish ray of sunlight gleamed in a clear blue patch of sky. Those gay animals greeted it with a friendly roar as they shook their wet hairy faces. I wanted to hug and kiss those two-legged beasts who worked so skilfully and deftly, so completely absorbed that they did not have a thought for themselves.

It seemed that nothing could withstand that joyful furious tempestuous surge of strength, that it was capable of working miracles on earth and of filling it overnight with beautiful palaces and cities, as it was told in prophetic fairy tales. After looking down on those toiling men for one or two minutes, the ray of sunlight failed to break through that dense bank of clouds and was drowned in it like a child in the sea. And now the rain turned into a heavy downpour.

'We can knock off now,' someone shouted, but he was angrily answered by the others: 'I'll knock *you* off!'

Right up to two o'clock, until the whole cargo had been loaded onto the other barge, those half-naked men worked without stopping in a torrential downpour and biting wind. All this made me understand with deep reverence what powerful forces enriched the world of men.

Afterwards they boarded the steamboat and they all fell fast asleep, as though they were drunk. When we reached Kazan they poured out onto the sandy shore in a grey muddy torrent and went off to a pub to drink the nine gallons of vodka.

The thief Bashkin came over to me in the pub and asked: 'What have they been doing to you?'

I gave him a rapturous account of the work. He listened to what I had to say, sighed and said in a disdainful voice: 'You fool! No, you're worse, you're an *idiyot*!'

He went away whistling, wriggling like a fish, and seemed to be swimming among the tightly packed tables, at which the stevedores sat noisily drinking and eating. Over in a corner someone started singing an obscene song:

> 'Oh, it happened at night time,
> A lady went a-walking in her garden . . .'

About ten voices joined in a deafening roar, beating their palms on the tables as he went on:

> 'The watchman was guarding the town
> He saw a lady a-lying on the ground . . .'

There were guffaws, whistles and thunderous words which, for their desperate cynicism, were probably unequalled anywhere in the world. Someone introduced me to Andrey Derenkov who owned a small grocery hidden away at the end of a poor, narrow little street overlooking a gully that was always piled high with rubbish.

Derenkov was a small kind-faced man with a withered arm, a fair beard and clever eyes. He possessed the best collection of banned and rare books in the town and they were used by students from the numerous scholastic establishments in Kazan and by various people of a revolutionary frame of mind.

Derenkov's shop was situated in a low lean-to built onto the house of a castrate money-lender. The door of the shop led into a large room which was dimly lit by one window looking out onto the yard. Behind this room was a cramped little kitchen and behind this, in a corner of a dark hall between the lean-to and the house, was a secret storeroom which housed the pernicious books. Some of the books had been copied in ink into thick notebooks, for example Lavrov's *Historical Letters*, Chernyshevsky's *What is to be done?*, a few articles by Pisarev, *Tsar Hunger*, and *Crafty Tricks*. All of these manuscripts were well thumbed and had been read again and again.

When I first went into the shop Derenkov was busy with some customers and he nodded towards the door into the back room. I entered it and saw a little old man kneeling in one corner and fervently praying in the dark. He reminded me of the portrait of Seraphim of Sarov. As I looked at him I felt there was something wrong, something contradictory. Derenkov had been described to me as a narodnik. I imagined a narodnik to be a revolutionary, but revolutionaries should not believe in God and that pious old man seemed out of place in that house. When he had finished praying he meticulously smoothed his white hair and beard, looked closely at me and said: 'I'm Andrey's father. Who are you? Really? And I thought you were a student in disguise.'

'Why should a student disguise himself?' I asked.

'Well,' the old man softly replied 'whatever you wear, God will find you out.'

He went into the kitchen while I sat by the window and was soon deep in thought. Suddenly I heard someone exclaim: 'That's him!'

A young girl dressed in white was standing by the kitchen

door. Her fair hair was cut short and blue eyes smiled from her pale, puffy face. She was just like an angel in a cheap print.

'Why are you so frightened? Surely I'm not so terrible?' she said in a fine, tremulous voice as she slowly and cautiously edged over to me, keeping close to the wall, as though she were not walking on solid ground at all, but along a shaky tightrope. This difficulty she had in walking made her resemble even more a being from some other world.

She was trembling all over, as though someone were sticking needles into her feet and the wall was burning her child-like, puffy hands. Her fingers were strangely motionless.

I stood in silence in front of her and felt a strange embarrassment mingled with deep pity. Everything in that dark room was out of the ordinary!

She sat on a chair so carefully as though she was afraid it would fly away from under her. Simply, unlike anyone else, she told me that she had been up and about only five days and that before then she was bedridden for nearly three months: she had lost the use of her arms and legs. 'It was some kind of nervous disease,' she said, smiling.

I remember feeling that I wanted her illness to be explained in some other way: a nervous disease was far too prosaic to account for *that* girl in a strange room where everything clung timidly to the walls, where the ikon lamp burned too brightly and where the shadow of its copper chains flickered over the white cloth on the large dinner table for no apparent reason. 'I've heard a lot about you,' she said in a thin, child-like voice. 'That's why I wanted to see what you were like.'

This girl gave me a look that I found unbearable and she seemed to be reading right through me with those piercing blue eyes.

I just did not know how to speak to someone like her. So I said nothing, and looked at the portraits of Herzen, Darwin and Garibaldi.

A young boy, about my age and with tow-coloured hair and impudent eyes, dashed out from the shop, shouted in a brittle voice, 'What are you doing here, Marya?' and disappeared into the kitchen.

'That's my youngest brother, Aleksey,' the girl said. 'I was training to be a midwife, but then I suddenly became ill. Why don't you say something? Are you shy?'

Andrey Derenkov arrived with his withered arm stuck into the front of his shirt. He silently stroked his sister's soft hair, ruffled it and then asked what kind of work I was looking for.

Then a young girl with reddish curls, a good figure and greenish eyes appeared. She looked at me forbiddingly, took the girl in white by the arm and led her away with the words: 'That's enough, Marya.'

The name did not suit her – it was too coarse.

I left as well, with a peculiar feeling of agitation, and a day later, during the evening, I was sitting in that room once again trying to fathom out what sort of lives people lived there, and how. But, strangely, they did live there.

That gentle, lovable white-headed old Stepan Ivanovich – so pale it seemed that he was transparent – was sitting in one corner and peering out, moving his dark lips and gently smiling as though he were asking: 'Don't touch me!'

He was as timid as a hare and I could clearly see that he was filled with an uneasy feeling of impending disaster.

Andrey, with his withered arm, and his grey jacket, the front thick with grease and with flour that had dried and become as stiff as the bark of a tree, sidled up and down the room with a guilty smile on his face – like a child that had just been forgiven some mischief.

Alexei, who was a lazy, rough boy, used to help him in the shop. The third brother, Ivan, was studying at a teachers' training college and, since he was a boarder, came home only on holidays. He was a small, smartly dressed, well-groomed young man, rather like an ageing civil servant. His invalid sister Marya lived upstairs in some attic and rarely came down. But when she did come I felt awkward, as though someone were binding me with invisible chains.

The Derenkov household was run by a tall, lean woman with a face like a wooden doll and with the stern eyes of a spiteful nun. She was the mistress of the castrate-landlord. And there was her red-haired daughter Nastya whose nostrils would twitch when she looked at men with her green eyes. But the people who had most say in that house were students from the University, the theological academy and the veterinary institute. They were a noisy crowd and they never stopped worrying about the Russian people and were perpetually anxious about the future of the country. They were always excited by articles they had seen in daily newspapers, conclusions in books they had just read, by all that was happening in the town and university, and they used to come from every street in Kazan to gather in Derenkov's shop and have heated arguments or whisper quietly to each other in the corners of the room. They would bring thick books with them and shout at each other as they poked their fingers at different passages to defend whichever truths happened to appeal to them.

Naturally, I did not understand what they were arguing about and the truths they affirmed were lost for me in that stream of words, like little globules of fat melting in watery soup given to the poor. Some of the students reminded me of old bible scholars from the different sects who lived along the Volga. But I could see that here were people who were ready to change life for the better, and although the sincerity of what they said was sometimes smothered in their turbulent flow of words, it did not drown. I clearly saw the problems that they were trying to solve and I felt personally involved in their successful solution. It often struck me that my own inarticulate thoughts found proper expression in the words of those students and I felt great enthusiasm for these people, just like a prisoner promised his freedom.

And they looked on me like carpenters examining a piece of wood which could be fashioned into something rather out of the ordinary.

When they introduced me to each other they said approvingly: 'He's got natural ability,' and they said this with the pride of street urchins showing off copper coins that they had found on the pavement. I did not like being described in this way, nor did I like 'son of the people' and I felt I was an outcast: I often felt very keenly the heavy weight of the forces that were guiding my mental development.

Once, when I saw a book in a shop window with a title consisting of words I had never seen before: 'Aphorisms and Maxims', I was seized by a burning desire to read it and I asked a student from the theological academy to get it for me. 'Well, now,' replied the future archbishop – a boy with the head of a negro, curly hair, thick lips and protruding teeth, '*that*, my friend, is a load of rubbish. You read what you're given and don't go poking your nose into things that don't concern you!'

I was hurt by this rude answer. Of course, I bought the book, partly with some money I earned on the wharves, having borrowed the rest from Andrey Derenkov. This was the first serious book that I had ever bought and I have it to this day.

On the whole they were rather strict with me. When I read the 'Alphabet of the Social Sciences' it struck me that the part played by pastoral tribes in cultural life was exaggerated by the author and that he had insulted enterprising tramps and hunters. When I communicated these doubts to a philologist, he tried to make his woman's face look impressive and lectured me for a whole hour about the 'right to criticize'.

'In order to have the right to criticize you must believe in some sort of truth or other. What do *you* believe in?'

He even read books in the street and he would walk along the pavement with his face buried in one, so that he bumped into people. As he lay tossing in his attic from starving typhus he would shout: 'Morality should be a harmonious synthesis of freedom and necessity . . . har-har-m . . .'

A gentle man, whom chronic malnutrition had made a semi-invalid and who was worn out by stubbornly pursuing a lasting truth, he knew no other joy in life except reading, and his tender dark eyes would smile happily, just like a child, when he thought that he had reconciled the contradictions of two powerful minds. Ten years after my life in Kazan I met him in Kharkov, where he was once again studying at the university after serving five years' exile in Kem. He seemed to be living in an ant-hill of conflicting thoughts. Although he was dying from tuberculosis, he was still trying to reconcile Marx and Nietzsche, coughing up blood and wheezing as he gripped my hands with his cold, clammy fingers: 'Life without *synthesis* is impossible!'

He died in a tram on the way to the university.

He was one of many martyrs to reason I had known and their memory is sacred to me.

About twenty similarly-minded people used to meet at the Derenkovs' and there was even a Japanese by the name of Panteleymon Sato, who was studying at the theological academy. He was a big man with a broad chest and he had a thick, flowing beard. His head was shaven Tartar fashion, and he seemed to be tightly sewn up in his grey Cossack jacket which was hooked right up to his chin. Usually he would sit in one corner puffing away at his short pipe, calmly surveying everyone with his grey, penetrating eyes, which often riveted themselves on me and made me feel that this serious man was mentally weighing me up, and for some reason I was afraid of him. I was astonished by his long silences. Everyone else spoke a great deal, in loud determined voices, and naturally, the sharper the things they said, the more I liked them.

But it was a long time before I guessed how often these remarks concealed pathetic, hypocritical ideas. What lay behind *that* bearded hero's long silences?

They called him Tufty and apparently no one except Andrey knew his real name. I soon discovered that he had only recently returned from exile in the Yakutsk region, where he had been for ten years. This made me even more interested in him, but it did not give me the courage to try and get to know him, although I was not a shy person; on the contrary. I was consumed by a restless curiosity, a thirst for knowing every-thing in the shortest possible time. This is a side of my char-acter that has prevented me all my life from devoting myself seriously to any one thing. When they spoke to me about the common people I felt amazed and it destroyed my self-confi-dence when I realized that I could not think the same way on this subject as they did. For them the people were the living embodiment of wisdom, spiritual beauty and kindness, almost god-like and consubstantial, the foundation of all that was beautiful, just and sublime. But I had never known any people who were really like this. I had seen carpenters, steve-dores, bricklayers, men like Yakov, Osip, Grigory, and yet these students were talking about the people as though they were of the same substance as God, while they placed them-selves on a lower level, dependent on their will. And it struck me that it was precisely men like these students who embodied beauty and power of thought, and in whom was concentrated a burning, noble, philanthropic will to spend their lives re-constructing life, unhampered, along some new, humani-tarian lines.

It was just this love of humanity that I could never find in the miserable specimens among whom I had lived up to this time, but here it resounded in every word, glowed in every look.

The speeches of these populists fell on my heart like re-freshing rain and all that naive literature about wretched vil-lage life, about the martyr–peasant, helped me a great deal. I came to feel that it was only through a very strong and pas-sionate love of man that one could gain the necessary strength to discover and understand the meaning of love. I stopped thinking about myself and began to pay more attention to others.

Andrey Derenkov told me in confidence that all the modest income from his shop was used to help these people who be-lieved above all in 'the happiness of the people'. He buzzed around them, just like a deeply pious deacon in his episcopal duties, and he never concealed his delight at the ready wisdom of those bookworms. He would smile happily, stick his withered arm in his shirt, tug his soft little beard in all directions with his other and ask me: 'Was it good? Oh, yes, yes!'

And whenever the veterinary surgeon Lavrov – a man with a strange voice like a cackling goose – came out with heretical remarks about the populists, Derenkov would cover up his eyes in fright and whisper: 'He's a real trouble-maker!'

He held the same opinion of the populists as myself, but the way the students treated him struck me as crude and condescending, just like master and workman, or innkeeper and waiter. He himself did not notice this. When he had seen the guests out he would often make me stay the night. We would clean the room up and then lie on thick felt mats on the floor, amicably whispering to each other for a long time in the darkness which was barely lit by the little flame of the lamp. He used to tell me, with the quiet joy of the true believer, that 'Hundreds, thousands of these good people will rise up one day and will take over the most important positions in Russia and change our way of life at one stroke!'

He was ten years older than me and I could see that he liked Nastya the red-head very much. He tried not to look into her eager eyes and when people were present talked to her in the dry, commanding tone of a master, but at the same time looked at her longingly. When he was alone with her he smiled in an embarrassed, timid way and tugged his beard. His little sister used to watch the verbal battles from a corner as well. Her child-like face puffed up comically and her eyes opened wide in her effort to follow what was going on, and when especially sharp words rang out she would sigh out loud, just as though she had been sprinkled with iced water.

The sandy-haired medical student walked up and down in front of her like a solemn cockerel. He spoke to her in a mysterious half-whisper, and tried to inspire her by frowning. All this was extraordinarily interesting. But autumn drew near and life without steady work became unbearable for me. Since

I was so carried away by everything that was going on around me I worked less and less. And I found another's bread was always very difficult to swallow. I would have to find a situation for the winter and I found it in Vasiliy Semyonov's pretzel bakery.

This period of my life is outlined in my stories: *The Boss*, *Konovalov*, and *Twenty six men and one girl* – a difficult time! However, it was instructive.

It was difficult physically and even more so *morally*.

When I went down into the bakehouse cellar a 'wall of oblivion' reared up between myself and the people, the sight and sound of whom had become a necessity for me. None of them ever came into the bakehouse to see me and since I had to work fourteen hours a day I was unable to visit Derenkov on weekdays. On holidays I either slept or stayed with my workmates. From the beginning some of them looked on me as an amusing clown, while others treated me with the naive love of children for someone who could tell interesting stories. The devil alone knows what I said to these people, but it goes without saying I told them everything that might inspire them with the hope that life would be different, easier and more meaningful. Sometimes I succeeded and when I saw those puffy faces shine with the sadness of humanity, while their eyes glinted with a sense of injury and anger, it put me in a festive mood and I proudly thought that I was really 'working among the people' and 'educating' them.

But, of course, it was more often the case that I sensed my own impotence, ignorance and inability to answer even the simplest questions of life, about the things around me. Then I felt that I had been thrown into a dark pit where people were swarming like blind-worms, trying to forget reality and finding oblivion in pubs and in the cold embraces of prostitutes. Visiting brothels each month on payday was obligatory. The men would have waking dreams about this pleasure a week before the happy day and when it had passed would spend hours telling each other about the delights they had experienced. In these conversations they would boast cynically of their virility, make cruel fun of women, spitting disgustedly when they spoke about them.

But strange to say, behind all this I could detect – or thought I could – sorrow and shame. I could see that my friends felt awkward and guilty in these 'houses of comfort' where for a rouble one could buy a woman for a whole night, and this struck me as only natural. But some of them were *too* free and easy and behaved with a boldness behind which I could see deliberation and deceit. I was keenly interested in the relations between the sexes and I watched them particularly closely.

I myself had not yet enjoyed a woman's embrace and my abstinence put me in an unpleasant position – both women and male friends cruelly mocked me. Soon they stopped inviting me to the 'house of comfort' and told me quite bluntly: 'Don't come with us, friend.'

'Why not?'

'Well! We don't like it with you around!'

I grasped at these words and felt there was something important in them for me, but they did not make anything clearer.

'You're a one, you are! We've told you not to come! It's no fun with you around!'

Only Artem said with a smile: 'It's as though we had a priest with us, or our own father.' At first the girls laughed at my reserve, but then they began asking me in offended voices: 'Too squeamish?'

The voluptuous and beautiful Tereza Boruta, a Polish girl of forty and a 'housekeeper', looked at me with the intelligent eyes of a pedigree dog and said: 'Leave him alone, girls, he must have a fiancée, yes? A strong boy like him *must* have a girl.'

She was an alcoholic, and was indescribably revolting when she was drunk. When she was sober, however, she amazed me by her concern for people and her calm search for some logic in what they did.

'Just can't make that lot out, must be students from the Academy, oh yes,' she said to my friends. 'This is what they do to girls: they smear the floor with soap, make a naked girl go down on all fours with plates under her hands and legs, then they give her a push in the behind and see how far she'll slide. Yes, one after the other. *Why* do they do it?'

'You're lying,' I said.

'Oh, no!' Tereza exclaimed without taking offence, and with a calmness that had something overpowering in it.

'You made it up!'

'How could a young girl like me do that? Do you think I'm mad?' she said, opening her eyes wide.

People listened to our argument with hungry attention, while Tereza went on telling her stories about the games her visitors played in the dispassionate tone of a person in search of one thing only: to understand *why*.

The audience spat in disgust, and swore wildly at the students. But since I saw that Tereza aroused hostility towards people whom I had come to love, I replied that the students loved the common people and wished them only good.

'Yes, these are students from Voskresensky Street, civilians from the university. But I'm talking about students *in orders*, from the Arsky Field! They're all orphans. But orphans grow into thieves or mischief makers, bad people, without any ties. That's orphans for you!'

Those calm stories told by the 'housekeeper' and the malicious complaints of the girls against the students, civil servants, and the 'pure public' in general, aroused not only hostility and repulsion in my friends but something that was almost joy as well, and this was expressed in the words: 'That means the ones with education are worse than us!'

Listening to such words was oppressive and bitter for me. I could see that all the filth in the city was flowing into the half-lit, tiny rooms, just as though they were pits, boiling up in a foul smoky fire there, and when it was saturated with hostility and malice it poured out into the city again. In these little holes, into which people were driven by instinct and boredom, touching songs were made up from stupid words about the anxieties and torments of love, ugly legends arose about the life of 'educated people' and a mocking, hostile attitude towards what they did not understand was born. And I could see that 'houses of comfort' were in fact universities, where my friends acquired knowledge of a very venomous kind.

I watched the 'girls of joy' lazily shuffling their feet across the dirty floor, their flabby bodies shaking repulsively to the wearisome screeching of the accordion or the exasperating rattling of a broken piano. I watched, and I began to be filled with vague but alarming thoughts.

Boredom seeped out of everything around me, poisoning my soul with the impotent desire to go off somewhere.

When I started telling the men in the workshop that there were those who were disinterestedly seeking roads to freedom, to happiness for the people, they retorted: 'But the girls don't say *that* about them!' And they mocked me mercilessly, with a cynical malice. I was an eager puppy though, and I considered myself no more stupid – more daring, in effect – than fully-grown dogs; and I could get angry as well. So I came to understand that reflecting on life was no less wearying than life itself; there were times when I felt flashes of hatred in my soul towards those stubbornly patient people with whom I worked. I was particularly disturbed by their capacity for suffering, the hopeless resignation with which they succumbed to the half-mad insults of our drunken employer.

And – almost by design – in those difficult times I became acquainted with a completely new idea, and although this was fundamentally alien to my way of thinking it nonetheless disturbed me deeply.

On one of those stormy nights when it seemed that the wind, with its vicious howling, had torn the grey sky into the tiniest shreds, scattering them over the earth and burying it under drifts of frozen dust, and when it seemed that all life on

47

earth was over, that the sun had gone out and would never rise again – on one of these Shrovetide nights I was returning to the workshop from the Derenkovs. As I battled along against the wind through that turbid, seething grey chaos, I tripped up over a man who was lying across the pavement. We both swore at each other – I in Russian and he in French: 'Oh, *diable*!'

This aroused my curiosity. I lifted him up and set him on his feet. He was not tall and did not weigh much. He pushed me away and shouted furiously: 'My hat, blast you! Give me my hat. I'll freeze!'

I found the hat in the snow, shook it, and put it back on his bristly head. But he tore it off, waved it about, swore in French and Russian and started driving me away with the words: 'Clear off!'

Then he suddenly threw himself forwards and was swallowed up in the seething mass. A little way on I saw him again. There he was, embracing the wooden post of a street lamp, and he said convincingly: 'Lena, I'm dying. Lena . . .'

He was obviously drunk and would have frozen if I had left him there in the street. I asked him where he lived.

'What street is this?' he asked with tears in his voice. 'I don't know where to go.'

I grasped him round the waist and led him away, trying to find out where he lived. 'On the Bulak,' he muttered shivering. 'On the Bulak, where there's baths, houses . . .' He walked uncertainly, stumbling and getting in my way. I could hear his teeth chattering.

'*Si tu savais*,' he muttered, pushing me.

'What did you say?'

He stopped, lifted his arm and said distinctly – and with pride in his voice, or so it seemed: '*Si tu savais, ou je te mène*.'

He thrust his fingers into his mouth, staggered and almost fell. I squatted, lifted him onto my back and carried him off. He pressed his cheek to my head and growled '*Si tu savais* – but I'm freezing, oh God!'

When we got to the Bulak I persuaded him to tell me, with great difficulty, which house he lived in. Finally we stumbled into the entrance of a small wing hidden in the swirling snow at the back of a courtyard. He groped for the door, knocked cautiously and whispered: 'Sh-sh, quiet!'

The door was opened by a woman in a red dressing-gown with a burning candle in one hand. Without saying a word she let us in, moved to one side, took out a lorgnette from somewhere and started looking me up and down. I told her that the man's hands seemed to be frozen stiff and that he must be undressed and put to bed.

'Do you think so?' she asked in a young, sonorous voice.

'We must soak his hands in cold water.'

She silently pointed towards one corner with her lorgnette. An easel was standing there with a painting of a river and trees. I looked with amazement into the woman's peculiarly motionless face. She walked over to a table in the corner, on which a lamp with a pink shade was burning. She sat down, picked up the jack of hearts and began staring at it.

I asked very loudly, 'Do you have any vodka?', but she did not answer and laid the cards out on the table. The man sat on a chair with his head hung low and his red hands lying on his body. I laid him on the couch and started undressing him, not understanding what was happening, just as though I were dreaming. The wall in front of me was entirely covered with photographs and in the middle was a tarnished golden wreath with white ribbons round it, at the end of which the gilt letters: 'To the incomparable Dzhilda' were printed.

'Careful, damn you!' the man groaned when I started rubbing his hands.

The woman continued laying the cards out, silently, and with a worried look on her face. She had a sharp, bird-like nose and her large motionless eyes lit up her face. Then with the hands of a young girl she ruffled up her grey hair which was so luxuriant it looked like a wig and she asked in a soft but rich voice: 'Have you seen Misha, Georges?'

Georges pushed me to one side, quickly sat down and hurriedly said: 'But you know he's gone to Kiev.'

'Yes, to Kiev,' the woman repeated without taking her eyes off the cards. I noticed that her words were all pitched in the same key and that her voice was absolutely devoid of expression.

'He'll be back soon.'

'Really?'

'Oh yes, very soon.'

'Really?' she repeated.

Half-dressed as he was Georges leaped onto the floor, and in two little jumps was kneeling at the woman's feet and speaking in French.

'I'm not worried,' she answered in Russian.

'Did you know that I got completely lost? There was a blizzard, a terrible wind, and I thought that I would freeze to death' Georges said this hurriedly and looked at her hand which was lying on her knee. He was about forty and his red, thick-lipped face with its black moustache was frightened and worried.

He rubbed hard at the patch of grey hair on his round skull and spoke more and more soberly.

'Tomorrow we are leaving for Kiev,' the woman said in a voice which was neither questioning nor affirmative.

'Yes, tomorrow! But you must rest first. Why don't you lie down? It's very late . . .'

'Won't Misha be coming today?'

'No. The storm's too bad. Come on, lie down . . .'

He took the lamp from the table and led the woman through a small door behind the book cupboard.

For a long time I sat there on my own and without thinking about anything as I heard his soft, rather hoarse voice. Hairy paws scraped over the window panes. The candle flame was weakly reflected in a pool of melted snow. The room was crammed with all sorts of things and it was filled with a strange warm smell that made me feel drowsy.

Then Georges reappeared. He staggered as he carried the lamp in his hand and its shade made a knocking sound on the window.

'She's gone to bed.'

He put the lamp back on the table, stopped in the middle of the room, looked very thoughtful for a moment and then started speaking without looking at me: 'Well, what do you make of it? I would have died if it hadn't been for you. Thanks! Who *are* you?'

He leaned his head to one side, listened to a rustling sound in the next room, and then he shuddered.

'Is that your wife?' I asked softly.

'Yes, that's my wife, she's all I have!' He said this in a soft clear voice, looking at the floor, and once again started rubbing his head with the palms of his hands.

'Like a cup of tea?' I asked.

Then he absently went towards the door, but before he reached it he stopped, remembering that the cook had eaten too much fish and had been taken to hospital.

I suggested putting the samovar on for him and he nodded. It was clear that he had forgotten that he was half-dressed and his feet shuffled over the damp floor as he took me into the little kitchen. He leaned with his back to the stove and repeated what he had said before: 'If it hadn't been for you I would have frozen. Thanks!'

Then he shuddered and stared at me with wide open eyes that were full of fear: 'What would have happened to her *then*? Oh, God . . .'

As he looked at the little black patch of the door, he said in a rapid whisper: 'You can see she's not well. Her son shot himself. He was a musician in Moscow and she's been waiting for him to come back for nearly two years now . . .'

Afterwards, when we were drinking tea, he told me incoherently, and in very strange words, that the woman was a landowner and that he had been history tutor to her son. He had fallen in love with her and she left her German husband, who was a baron and sang in the opera. They lived very well, although her first husband had done everything he could to ruin her life.

He spoke with his eyes screwed up, closely staring at something in the half light of the dirty kitchen where the floor had rotted through by the stove. He scalded himself sipping the tea, his face wrinkled up and his round eyes blinked in fear.

'Who *are* you?' he asked once more. 'Yes, I know, a pretzel baker, a labourer. Strange . . . it doesn't suit you. Why is this?'

His voice was agitated and he glanced at me suspiciously, with a persecuted look.

In a few words I told him about myself.

'Really, so that's it?' he exclaimed softly. 'Well . . .'

Then he suddenly livened up and asked: 'Do you know the story about the ugly duckling? Have you read it?'

His face became distorted, and his voice sounded furious, amazing me by its unnatural pitch, almost like a scream.

'Those fairy tales can be tempting. When I was your age I too wondered whether I would become a swan. I was supposed to enter the Academy and then the University. My father was a priest and he disowned me. I went to Paris and studied the history of humanity's misfortunes – the history of progress. Yes, I even wrote about it. Oh, how it all . . .'

He jumped up in his chair, listened hard and said: 'Progress has only been invented as a means of comforting oneself. Life is stupid, without any meaning. There is no progress without slavery and without the subjugation of the majority to the minority, humanity has stopped dead in its tracks. Because we wish to make life easier we only make things more difficult, forcing ourselves to work harder. Factories and machines exist only to make more and more machinery. That's so stupid! There are more and more factory workers all the time, but all we need is the peasant, someone who produces bread. Bread – that is all one must strive to take from nature. The less men need the happier they are. But the more they desire, the less freedom they have.'

Perhaps these were not the exact words, but this was the first time I had heard these stunning phrases, and expressed so sharply, in such an undisguised form.

Then he cried out excitedly, anxiously rested his eyes on the door that opened into the inner rooms, listened to the silence for a moment and then whispered, almost in a frenzy: 'You must understand that no one needs much to live on – a piece of bread and a woman . . .'

When he spoke about women in that mysterious whisper, with words that were unknown to me, quoting poetry that I had not read, he suddenly resembled Bashkin the thief.

'Beatrice, Fiametta, Laura, Ninon,' he whispered, names that were unfamiliar to me. He told me about some kings and poets who were in love and read French poetry to me, beating out the metre with his thin arm which was bare to the elbow.

'The world is ruled by love and hunger,' he eagerly whispered and I remembered that these were the words printed under the title of the revolutionary pamphlet *Tsar Hunger*, and this lent them considerable significance, in my opinion.

'People seek oblivion, comfort, but not knowledge!'

This last thought completely stunned me.

It was morning when I left the kitchen – the little clock on the wall showed just past six and I wandered in the grey mist among snowdrifts, listening to the sound of the storm, recalling the fiendish screams of that broken man, and I felt that his words had stuck somewhere in my throat and were choking me. I did not want to go back to the workshop to see people. With the snow heavy on my coat I roamed around the Tartar district until dawn came and the people of the town began to appear among the drifted snow. I did not meet that teacher again, nor did I want to. But I subsequently often heard similar speeches about the meaninglessness of life and the futility of work – speeches made by illiterate wanderers, homeless tramps, followers of Tolstoy, and highly cultured people. The same thing was said by a priest, a Master of Divinity, a chemist who worked on explosives, a new vitalist biologist and by many others. But these words no longer had the shattering effect they had before, when I first got to know them. And only two years ago – thirty years since I had my first discussion on these topics – did I unexpectedly hear those very same ideas again, expressed in almost exactly the same words by a workman who was an old friend of mine.

Once again I had a 'heart-to-heart' with him and this man who called himself, gloomily smiling, a 'bigwig in politics' told me with that impassive sincerity which apparently only Russians possess: 'My dear Aleksei Maximovich, I don't need anything. All those academies, sciences, aeroplanes lead nowhere, they're all *too* much. All I need is a quiet little home, a woman whom I can kiss when I want to and who would be faithful to me in spirit and body. You talk just like those intellectuals. No, you're not one of us any more. You've been poisoned. For you ideas mean more than men. You think like those Jews, that man was created for the Sabbath.'

'Jews don't think that.'

He threw the stub of his cigarette into the river, watched it float away and said: 'I'm damned if I know what they really think, can't make them out at all . . .'

We sat on a granite seat on one of the quays along the Neva. It was a moonlit autumn night. Both of us were worn out by a day of stupid worries, by our stubborn but unavailing desire to do something good and helpful for mankind. He continued in a quiet, pensive voice: 'You're *with* us, but you're not one of us, that's what I'm saying. Intellectuals like worrying, they've supported revolutions from time immemorial. Like Christ, who was an idealist and rebelled for the sake of ideas that were beyond this world, the intellectuals rebel for the sake of some Utopia. The idealist rebels, and all the nonentities, rabble, scum, join him. And it's out of spite, because they see that there is no place in life for them. The working man rebels for the revolution. What he wants is a just distribution of tools and products of labour. Once he has finally achieved power do you think that he would agree to a State? Not for anything! He will go his own way and each one of them will find himself a quiet little place... Did you mention *technology*? It pulls the noose around our necks even tighter. No, we must free ourselves from unnecessary labour, man needs peace of mind. Factories and science don't provide it. A man needs very little for himself. Why should I try to build a whole town when all I need is a little house? Where people live on top of each other there is running water, sewerage and electricity. But if you tried to live without all that how easy life would be! No, we have far too much and it all comes from the intelligentsia. That's why I say the intelligentsia are a harmful lot.'

I told him that no nation was capable of making life so decidedly meaningless as we Russians.

'Spiritually, they are the freest people,' he said grinning. 'Only don't get angry, I'm right in saying that millions think the same but they don't know how to express themselves. Life must be made simpler, then it will treat people more charitably.'

This man had never been a follower of Tolstoy, never showed any leaning towards anarchism. I knew the story of his spiritual development very well. After my talk with him I could not help thinking: what if it were true that millions of Russians only suffer the terrible tortures of revolution because in the depths of their hearts they cherish the hope of being liberated from their toil? The minimum of work, the maximum of enjoyment – that is all very alluring and seductive, like everything that is impossible to realize, like all utopias.

And I remembered Ibsen's lines:

'Am I a conservative? Oh, no!
I am still the same as I have been all my life,
I don't like moving the pieces from one square to another,
I would like to move the whole game.
I can remember only one revolution
It was more clever than those that came after
And it could have destroyed everything
– I mean, of course, the Flood.

'But then the Devil himself was duped,
And Noah became Dictator.
Oh, if only I could do it more honourably,
I would not refuse you help.
If you struggled for a universal flood,
I would gladly put a torpedo under the Ark!'

Derenkov's shop did not bring much money in – the number of people and 'small businesses' needing financial help grew every day.

'We must think of something,' Andrey said as he stroked his beard anxiously. Then he would smile guiltily and sigh deeply.

It struck me that this man was convinced that he had been sentenced to life imprisonment in the service of others, and that although he was reconciled to this punishment, it was a great burden to him at times.

More than once, using different approaches, I would ask: 'Why do you do all this?'

It was obvious that he did not understand my questions, would answer my question 'Why?' as though he were reading from a book and he spoke unintelligibly about the hard life of the people, about the need for enlightenment, knowledge.

'But *do* people really desire and search for knowledge?' I asked.

'What do you mean? Of course they do! Don't *you*?'

Yes, I wanted knowledge. But I remembered the words of the history teacher. 'People seek oblivion, consolation – but not knowledge.'

These incisive ideas are only distorted when people over seventeen get hold of them: they become blunted and the young people themselves are the losers.

I realized that I was always seeing one and the same thing: people liked interesting stories only because they helped them forget momentarily their own lives which were in fact hard, but to which they had grown accustomed. The more fiction they found in a story, the more hungrily they listened to it.

Those books which had a great deal of fine 'inventiveness' interested them most. To put it briefly, I was swimming in a stupefying fog.

Derenkov hit upon the idea of opening a bakery. I remember that he had everything carefully worked out and that the business was bound to bring in not less than 35 per cent profit for every rouble invested. I had to work as the baker's 'assistant' and since I was 'one of them' I had to watch out that this baker did not steal any flour, eggs, butter or finished goods. And now I moved from a large dirty cellar into one that was smaller, but cleaner, and it was my job to keep it clean. Instead of a workman's guild of forty, I only had one worker under me. He had grey temples, a pointed beard, a lean, swarthy face, dark, pensive eyes and a strange mouth – it was small, just like a perch's, with fat puffy lips pursed in such a way that he seemed to be kissing himself mentally.

There was something mocking in the depths of his glinting eyes. Of course he was a thief and the very first night he hid ten eggs, three pounds of flour and a large chunk of butter in some corner.

'Who's all that lot for?' I asked.

'It's for some little girl,' he replied in a friendly voice. Then he crinkled the bridge of his nose and added: 'Yes, a fi-ine girl!'

I tried to convince him that stealing was a crime. But either because I was lacking in powers of oratory, or because I myself was not sufficiently sure of what I was trying to prove, my words had no effect.

As he lay on a bin full of dough and stared through the window at the stars, the baker suddenly muttered in amazement: 'So *he's* lecturing *me*! The first time he sees me he's already trying to teach me. He's three times younger than me, it's a laugh!'

He peered at the stars again and asked: 'Haven't I met you somewhere before? Who did you work for? Semyonov? Where the riots were? Oh . . . then I must have dreamed it . . .'

A few days later I noticed that this man could sleep indefinitely, in any position, even standing propped up against a spade. When he fell asleep he raised his eyebrows, his face changed mysteriously and took on an expression of ironic amazement. But his favourite topic was stories about hidden treasure, and dreams. He exclaimed convincingly: 'I can see right through the earth. It's crammed full with treasure, like a pie. There's lots of money, chests, cast iron pots everywhere. More than once I've dreamed of some familiar place – a bathroom, for example – with a trunk full of silver plates buried in one corner. I would wake up and go digging in the middle of the night. I would go two feet down and see cinders and a dog's skull. Yes, there it was ... I'd found it! Suddenly there would be a large crash and the window was shattered to smithereens. Then some old woman would start shouting like mad: "Police, burglars!" Of course, I would run away, otherwise they would beat me to death. It's a funny thing!'

I often heard him use that expression: 'It's a funny thing!' However, Ivan Kozmich Lutonin never laughed, but screwed up his eyes, wrinkled his forehead and puffed his nostrils out in a kind of smile. His dreams were very uncomplicated and as boring and absurd as reality itself. I could not understand how he could talk about his dreams so enthusiastically, when he never liked talking about all that was actually going on around him.*

One day the whole town was in a turmoil: the daughter of some rich tea merchant, forced to marry against her will, shot herself straight after the wedding. A few thousand young men and women followed her coffin. Students started making speeches at the graveside but the police drove them away. Everyone in that little shop next door to the bakery was shouting his head off about the tragedy and the room at the back of the shop was filled with students. Down in the cellar I could

* Author's note: At the end of the 1890s I read in some archaeological journal that Lutonin–Korovyakov had found treasure somewhere in the Chistopolsk region – a potful of Arabian coins.

hear excited voices and sharp words. 'They should have beaten her more when she was a young girl,' Lutonin was saying and then added in the next breath: 'I dreamed I was fishing for carp in a pond, when a policeman suddenly turned up. "Stop, how dare you?" There was nowhere to run to, so in I dived . . . and then I woke up.'

But although reality existed somewhere beyond the bounds of his consciousness he soon realized that there was something strange going on in the baker's shop, that young girls really unsuitable for the work were carrying on the business, people who read books – the master's sister and her friend, a big rosy-cheeked girl with warm eyes. Students would come there and sit for a long time at the back of the shop shouting or whispering about something. The master rarely came, but since I was his assistant everyone thought that I was in charge of the bakery.

'Are you related to the master?' Lutonin asked. 'Perhaps he sees you as a son-in-law. No? Then it's all very comical. But why do all those students hang around here? After the girls, I bet. Hm, that's possible, although they are nothing much to look at . . . Those scruffy students are more interested in fresh rolls than young ladies.'

Almost every day, at five or six in the morning, a girl with short legs would appear at the bakery windows. She seemed to be made up of little hemispheres of all sizes and looked just like a sack of water melons. She would yawn as she lowered her bare legs into the ditch in front of the window and called: 'Vanya!'

She wore a multi-coloured scarf and her bright curly hair escaped from under it, falling in little ringlets over her red cheeks that were inflated like rubber balls, and over her low forehead, tickling her sleepy eyes. She lazily brushed it back from her face with her little hands, keeping her fingers comically parted, like a new-born child. It was interesting to think: what could I say to a girl like her? I used to wake the baker up and he would ask her: 'So you've come, then?'

'You can see for yourself.'

'Have you been sleeping?'

'Well, what of it?'

'What did you dream about?'

'Can't remember.'

It was quiet in the town. But somewhere the silence was broken by the sound of a house porter sweeping and the chirruping of sparrows that had just woken up. The warm rays of the rising sun pressed against the window panes. I found these dreamy beginnings to the day very pleasant.

The baker would poke his hairy hand out of the window and feel the girl's legs. She accepted his advances indifferently and blinked her sheep-like eyes without even smiling.

'Peshkov, hurry up, it's time you took the pastry out.'

I would take the iron plates out of the stove and the cook would seize a dozen buns, puff pastries, rolls and throw them into the folds of the girl's skirt. She would toss a hot bun from one hand to the other, bite into it with her yellow sheep's teeth, burn herself in the process, moan slightly and mumble to herself angrily.

The baker would say admiringly: 'Let your skirt down, you little tart.' And when she left he would start showing off.

'Did you see that? Like a young lamb, covered in curls. I'm a decent man, my friend, I don't live with older women, only young girls. She's my thirteenth! She's Nikiforych's god-daughter.'

As I listened to his rapturous comments I would think: 'Should *I* live like that?' I used to take the white bread from the oven (sold by the pound), place ten or a dozen cottage loaves on a long board and hurry off with them to Derenkov's shop. When I got back I would fill a large basket with rolls and pastries and run off to the theological academy, in time for the students' morning tea. I used to stand at the door of that large dining hall and supply rolls 'on credit' and 'for cash'. And I would stay and listen to their arguments over Tolstoy. One of the professors from the Academy, Gusev, was a deadly enemy of Leo Tolstoy. Sometimes I carried books hidden under the rolls in my basket and I had to hand them over to some student without being seen. Sometimes the students would hide books or notes in my basket.

Once a week I would go even further, to the 'Madhouse', where the psychiatrist Bekhterev gave lectures, with the patients as subjects. Once he demonstrated a megalomaniac. When that tall man appeared at the door of the lecture room, wearing a white coat and a nightcap that resembled a sock, I could not help laughing. But he stopped for a moment as he passed me and peered into my face, which made me shrink back as though he had stabbed me in the heart with his black, but fiery, piercing look. And all through that lecture, while Bekhterev pulled his beard and respectfully chatted with his patient, I quietly stroked my face with the palm of my hand as though it had been scorched by burning dust.

The patient spoke in a deep, dull voice. He seemed to be asking for something as he menacingly stretched his long arm with its long fingers out of his dressing gown. It seemed that his whole body had become unnaturally elongated and was growing bigger and bigger, and I was convinced that he would grab hold of my throat with his swarthy hand from where he was standing. His dark eyes with their penetrating stare gleamed imperiously and menacingly from the dark pits in his bony face. About twenty students were observing this man in his absurd nightcap – some of them were smiling, but most of them looked on very attentively and sadly, and their eyes seemed particularly ordinary in comparison with his burning eyes. He was terrifying and there was definitely something majestic about him without any doubt!

The professor's voice rang out clearly against that fish-like silence of the students and each question produced terrible shouts from that deep, muffled voice, which seemed to be coming from under the floor, from the deathly, white walls. That patient's movements were as slow and solemn as an archbishop's.

At night I wrote some poetry about that megalomaniac and called him 'Master of masters, friend and counsellor of God.' For a long time visions of him lived with me and made life very difficult.

Since I had to work from six in the evening almost until the following afternoon, the only chance I had to read was during the day, in the middle of my work, after I had kneaded some dough and was waiting for another lot to turn sour and after the bread had been put into the oven.

The more I mastered the secrets of the trade the less the baker worked, and he would 'instruct' me, in a tone of friendly surprise: 'You are good at your work. In a year or two you'll be a master baker. It's a funny thing. You're still a young man, so no one does what you tell them or shows you any respect.'

He did not approve of my passion for books.

'You'd be better off sleeping than reading,' he advised me in a worried voice. But he never asked what books I read. He was completely obsessed with dreams of hidden treasure, and by that plump little girl. She often came at night and then he would either take her onto some sacks of flour at the front of the bakery, or, if it was cold, would wrinkle up the bridge of his nose and say to me: 'Go out for half an hour!'

I used to go out and think: How horribly different this love was from the kind they write about in books.

The master's sister lived in a little room at the back of the shop and I used to heat up samovars for her. But I tried to see her as little as possible, since she made me feel very uncomfortable. Her child-like eyes looked at me with the same unbearable stare as when we first met. Deep down in those eyes I suspected a smile and it seemed it was mocking me.

I was so overflowing with strength it made me clumsy. When the baker saw me dragging and rolling sacks weighing 180 pounds he would say sympathetically: 'You've the strength of three, but you're clumsy. Although you're tall, you're just like an ox . . .'

Despite the fact that I had already read many books, that I loved poetry and had started writing it myself, I always expressed myself 'in my own words'. I felt that they were heavy and harsh, but it seemed that it was only through them that I could express a great muddle of thoughts. But sometimes I deliberately used coarse words in protest against something that was alien to me and which irritated me. One of my teachers, a student mathematician, used to reproach me: 'The devil only knows what you use to express yourself. Not words, but iron weights!' On the whole I had little love for myself, something usually quite common with adolescents. I saw myself as comical, and crude. My face had high cheek-bones, like a Kalmyk, and my voice did not obey me.

In contrast the master's sister moved quickly and nimbly, like a swallow in the sky, and I thought that the ease with which she moved did not suit her plump, soft little body. There was something not quite right in the way she walked and her gestures that struck me as over-deliberate. She had a cheerful voice and she often laughed, and when I heard this ringing laugh I thought that she wanted me to forget what she had looked like the first time I saw her. But I had no wish to forget, since everything out of the ordinary was dear to me and I felt that I *had* to know that the unusual could, and did in fact, exist.

Sometimes she would ask me: 'What are you reading?'

I would give an answer briefly and I felt like asking: 'Why do you want to know?'

Once, when the baker was fondling the girl, he told me in a drunken voice: 'Go out for a few minutes. Yes, now you could be with the boss's sister – letting a chance like that slip! You students . . .'

I promised him that I would smash his head in with a weight if he said anything like that again and I went out into the hall where the sacks were. I could hear Lutonin's voice coming through a chink in the door which did not close properly.

'Why should I be angry with him? He's made himself drunk on books, lives like a madman.'

Rats squealed and scuttled about in the hall, while the young girl moaned and made cow-like noises in the bakehouse.

I went outside where a fine rain was falling lazily, almost silently. All the same it was close and the air was heavy with the smell of burning – the forests were on fire.

It was already long past midnight. The windows in the house opposite the bakery were open and I could hear people singing in the dimly lit rooms:

> 'St Varlamy himself
> With his golden head
> Looked down on them
> And smiled . . .'

I tried to picture Marya Derenkov when she lay on my lap, in the same way as the baker's girl lay on *his*, and I felt with all my being that this was impossible, even terrible.

> 'And all night along
> He drinks and sings
> And what else? Oh, he's busy
> With something or other . . .!'

The deep impassioned vowel 'O' could be heard above all other sounds. As I bent down with my hands on my knees I looked through the window. Through the lace curtains I could see a square pit, and its grey walls were lit by a tiny lamp with a light blue shade. A young girl with her face turned towards the window was sitting by it and writing. Suddenly she raised her head and with a red penholder smoothed back a lock of hair which had fallen down over her temple. Her eyes were screwed up and she was smiling. She slowly folded the letter, sealed the envelope with her tongue and threw it onto the table, pointing threateningly at it with a finger that was smaller than my little finger. Then she picked the letter up again, frowned, tore the envelope open, read the letter again, put it in another envelope, bent low over the table and wrote out an address. She waved it in the air like a white flag. Then she circled around with her arms clasped, went over to the corner where her bed was, and came away from it with her blouse off. Her shoulders were as round as doughnuts. She took a lamp from the table and disappeared into a corner. When one sees how people behave when they are all alone, then they appear to be insane. I walked round the yard thinking how strangely that girl behaved when she was by herself in her little lair.

But when the red-headed student with a voice as soft as a whisper came to see her and said something she stiffened up and seemed to shrink as she timidly surveyed him and hid her hands behind her back or under the table. I did not like him at all.

And now the baker's girl with her short legs stumbled by, muffled in a shawl, and she said: 'Get back into the bake-house.'

As the baker poured dough out of a bin he would tell me how comforting and tireless his beloved was, and this made me think: 'What's going to happen to me now?'

Business was so good that Derenkov was already looking for a larger bakery and decided to take on another assistant. This suited me well, since I had too much work to do and I would get tired to the point of stupefaction.

'You'll be the senior assistant in our new bakery,' the master promised me. 'I'll ask them to pay you ten roubles a month.'

I understood that it was to his advantage to have me as senior assistant. He did not like work, but I was a willing worker and found being tired had its advantages: it soothed my anxieties and restrained my persistent sexual urges. But it made reading impossible.

'It's a good thing you've given up books – the rats would have eaten them!' the baker said. 'But don't *you* ever have dreams? You must have, but you don't want to talk about them! It's a funny thing. You must agree that telling dreams

is the most harmless thing, there's nothing to be afraid of . . .'
He was very friendly towards me and it seemed that he even
respected me. Or perhaps he was frightened of me, since I was
the boss's protégé, although this did not prevent him from
systematically stealing goods from the shop.

Grandmother died. I only heard about her death seven
weeks after the funeral, in a letter from my cousin. In this
brief letter, totally lacking in commas, he wrote that while
Grandmother had been begging on a church porch she fell
and broke her leg. After eight days gangrene set in. Later I
learned that the two brothers, together with the sister with
her children – all healthy young people – had been living off
the money that Grandmother collected when she went begging. They did not have the sense to send for a doctor. My
cousin wrote: 'She was buried in the Petropavlovsk cemetery
where all the family followed the coffin and the beggars who
loved her and cried. Grandfather cried as well and drove us
away but stayed by the grave himself from some bushes we
watched him crying he will die soon.'

I did not cry, and all I remember is feeling that I had been
swept by an icy gust. At night, when I sat outside on a pile of
firewood, I felt a nagging desire to tell someone about Grandmother, how sincere and wise she was, a mother to all mankind.

This deep yearning stayed with me for a long while, but
since I had no one to whom I could open my heart, it eventually burnt itself out. I recalled these days many years later when
I read A. P. Chekhov's marvellously truthful story about a
cab-driver who talked to his horse about the death of his son.
And I deeply regretted that at that terribly difficult time I had
no horse or dog to talk to and that it never occurred to me to
share my grief with the rats – there were lots of them in the
bakehouse and I was on the best of terms with them.

Nikiforych the local constable started hovering over me
like a kite. He was an impressive-looking strong man with a
silvery bristle on his head, and a thick broad beard. He would

smack his lips with great relish and look at me just as though I were a goose killed for Christmas.

'Did I hear that you like reading?' he asked. 'What kind of books, for example? Lives of the saints or the Bible?'

I told him that I read both the Bible and the Daily Lessons.

He was amazed and clearly confused.

'Mm, really? Reading is useful – and legal! But have you never read the works of Count Tolstoy?'

I had read Tolstoy but apparently not those works that interested the policeman.

'These, for the sake of argument, are ordinary enough books that everyone seems to write. But they say that in others he took up arms against priests – you *should read them*!'

I had read those 'others' which were printed on a duplicating machine, but they struck me as boring and I knew that I had better not discuss them with the police.

After a few discussions we had while walking along, the old man began inviting me: 'Come over to my sentry box for a cup of tea.' Of course, I understood what he wanted from me, but I did not feel like going. So I took advice from some clever people and they decided that if I refused the policeman's hospitality this might make him view what was going on in the bakery more suspiciously. So I went to visit Nikiforych. A third of his little kennel was taken up by a Russian-style stove, and another by a double bed with chintz curtains round it. It was piled high with red calico cushions. The rest of the place was furnished with a crockery cupboard, two chairs and a bench by the window. Nikiforych unbuttoned his uniform, sat down on the bench, blocking the only small window with his body. Next to me was his wife, a large-bosomed woman of about twenty with a red face and crafty, evil-looking eyes that had a strange dove-like colour. Her bright red lips pouted impishly and her voice had a dry, malicious tone.

The policeman said: 'I have heard that my god-daughter Sekleteya visits you in the bakery. She's a loose, vile girl. All women are vile.'

'*All* of them?' his wife asked.

'Every single one!' he said convincingly, as he jangled his medals like a horse rattling its harness. Then he sipped some tea, and said, smacking his lips: 'Vile and dissolute right down to the last prostitute . . . even queens! The Queen of Sheba travelled about 1500 miles to see King Solomon just for an orgy. And the Empress Catherine, although she is called the Great . . .'

Then he gave a detailed account of some stoker who in the space of one night with the Empress had been awarded every rank from sergeant to general. His wife listened attentively, licking her lips and touching my foot under the table. Nikiforych spoke very smoothly, using appetising words and then, without my even noticing it, changed the subject: 'Now, for example, there's that first year student Pletnyov.'

His wife sighed and put in: 'Not good looking, but a nice boy!'

'Who?'

'Mr Pletnyov.'

'In the first place he is not a "Mr". He'll only be Mr Pletnyov when he finishes his course; in the meantime he's just a student, like thousands of others. In the second place, what do you mean by "nice"?'

'He's so cheerful. And young.'

'In the first place a circus clown is cheerful . . .'

'A clown gets paid for being cheerful.'

'Shut up! In the second place a male dog starts life as a puppy.'

'A clown is a kind of monkey.'

'Did you hear me say shut up? Did you?'

'Yes, I heard.'

'All right then.'

After Nikiforych had calmed his wife down he advised me: 'Now then, you must meet Pletnyov. He's a very interesting person.' As he had probably seen me with Pletnyov more than once in the street I told him: 'I know him already!'

'Really? Well then . . .

There was disappointment in his voice. He fidgeted violently and jangled his medals. But by now I was on my guard. I knew that Pletnyov had been printing certain pamphlets on a duplicating machine.

His wife touched my foot and craftily egged the old man on. He puffed himself up like a peacock and paraded words before me just like a peacock's tail with its rich feathers. His wife's little games made it hard to hear what he was saying and once again I failed to notice how his voice had changed, and had become softer and more persuasive.

'There's an invisible thread – do you understand?' he asked and looked into my face with rounded eyes, just as though something had frightened him! 'Now if you look on the Tsar as a *spider*.'

'Oh, you, what are you talking about?' his wife exclaimed.

'Shut up! You fool, I only said that to make my meaning clear, not as an insult. Clear the samovar away.'

He twitched his eyebrows, screwed his eyes up and carried on in the same persuasive voice: 'There's an invisible thread, like a spider's web, and it comes right out of his Imperial Majesty Alexander the Third's heart. And there's another which goes through all the ministers, through His Excellency the Governor and down through the ranks until it reaches me and even the lowest soldier. Everything is linked and bound together by this thread and with its invisible power it serves as a support, for centuries everlasting, for the Fatherland. But lousy little Poles, Jews and Russians, bribed by the cunning Queen of England, try to snap this thread wherever they can, pretending they're doing it for the people!' He leaned towards me over the table and asked in a menacing whisper: 'Do you *understand*? Why am I telling you all this? Your master-baker speaks highly of you, says you're clever and honest and that you live on your own. But students hang around your bakehouse and visit Derenkov's wife at night. Just one would be all right, but what when there's a lot of them? I've nothing

69

against students. One day someone's a student and the next he's a friend of the public prosecutor. Students are fine people, only they are in too much of a hurry to act some sort of part and they are encouraged by the enemies of the Tsar! Do you understand? And there's something else . . .'

But he did not manage to say any more, as the door flew wide open and in came a red-nosed little old man with a small band round his curly hair. He was carrying a bottle of vodka and he was already drunk.

'Care for a game of draughts?' he asked in a sprightly voice and immediately dazzled us with the sparks of his witty remarks.

'My father-in-law on the wife's side,' Nikiforych said in a gloomy, irritated voice.

A few minutes later I said good-bye and left. The crafty wife pinched me as she half-closed the door and said: 'Look at those red clouds. Just like a fire!'

There was just one small, fading gold-tinted cloud in the sky.

Without wishing to insult my teachers I must say that this policeman gave me a sharper, more graphic explanation of the whole State machinery than they did. Somewhere there was a spider which produced an 'invisible thread' which enmeshed the whole of life and bound it up. I soon learned to find the strong loops of this thread everywhere I went.

Late one evening, when the shop was shut, the master's wife called me over and told me, in a business-like voice, that she had instructions to find out what the policeman had been talking about. 'Oh God!' she exclaimed uneasily when she had heard my report. She scuttled like a mouse from one corner of the room to the other, shaking her head. 'Now tell me, has the baker been trying to get anything out of you? His mistress is related to Nikiforych, isn't she? We must get rid of him.'

I leaned against the door post and looked at her distrustfully. Somehow she had said 'mistress' too easily for my liking, and her decision to sack the baker did not exactly please me. 'You must be careful,' she said. As always, I was embarrassed by her persistent stare, which seemed to be asking me something that I could not understand. There she stood in front of me, with her arms behind her back.

'Why are you always so miserable?'

'I lost my grandmother not so long ago.'

This seemed to amuse her and she asked: 'Did you love her very much?'

'Yes . . . is there anything else you want?'

'No.'

I went out and that night I wrote some poetry in which, as far as I can remember, the following line kept on repeating itself: 'And you are not what you wish to appear.'

It was decided that the students should visit the bakery as little as possible. Since I did not see them now I almost completely lost the opportunity of inquiring about things I could not understand in books I had read and I started writing notes on questions that interested me in a notebook. However, once, when I was feeling tired, I fell asleep over my notes and the baker read them.

He woke me up and asked: 'What's this you're writing? "Why didn't Garibaldi drive the king out?" What's *Garibaldi*? And how can you drive a king out?' He angrily threw the book onto a flour bin, climbed down into a rainwater pit and growled: 'Tell me *why* he had to drive a king out! It's a funny thing. You must stop writing this fancy stuff. Too much reading! Five years ago in Saratov the gendarmes were arresting readers just like you, as though they were mice. Nikiforych has his eye on you enough already, without all this. Now you stop driving kings away, they're not doves!'

He meant well when he said this, but I could not reply in the way I wanted – I was forbidden to converse with the baker on 'dangerous topics'.

Some seditious book was being circulated round the town and it aroused a lot of argument. I asked Lavrov the veterinary surgeon to get it for me but he said in a hopeless voice: 'Oh no, not much chance of that, my friend! However, it looks like they're going to have readings from it at a certain place soon and perhaps I can take you there.' At midnight, on Assumption Day, I was striding across the Arsky Field, following Lavrov's figure in the darkness. He walked about three hundred yards in front of me. The field was deserted, but I made my way with 'due caution', as Lavrov had advised, whistling and singing and pretending to be a workman 'under the influence'.

Black wisps of cloud lazily floated above my head and among them the moon rolled around like a golden ball, shadows covered the earth and pools of water shone like silver and steel. Behind me I could hear the angry hum of the city.

My guide paused by the fence of some garden at the back of the theological academy and I hurriedly caught up with him. Without saying a word we climbed over the fence and went across the thickly overgrown garden, catching ourselves on branches, making large drops of water shower on us. We stopped by the wall of a house and softly tapped at the shutter of a tightly closed window, which was opened by a bearded man. Beyond him I could see only darkness and I could not hear a thing.

'Who's that?'

'We're from Yakov.'

'Come in.'

In that pitch-black darkness I could sense that many people were there. I could hear dresses rustling, feet shuffling, soft coughing and whispers. A match flared up, lighting my face, and I could make out several dark shapes sitting on the floor against the walls.

'Everyone here now?'

'Yes.'

'Draw the curtains so the light won't show through the shutters.'

An angry voice thundered: 'What smart alec thought we should all meet in an empty house?'

'Not so loud!'

In one corner someone lit a small lamp. The room was empty except for two boxes covered with a board, with five people sitting on it like jackdaws on a fence.

The lamp stood on one box, which had been turned upside down. Three more people were sitting on the floor by the wall and one very pale young man with long hair was perched on the window-sill. Apart from him and the bearded man I knew them all. The bearded man announced in a deep voice that he was going to read a paper called 'Our disagreements', written by George Plekhanov, who had been a member of the 'People's Will'. Someone sitting on the floor snarled in the darkness: 'We know all that!' The mysteriousness of the whole surroundings pleasantly excited me: the poetry of mystery is the highest poetry. I felt like some worshipper at morning service in a temple and I thought of catacombs, the first Christians. The room was filled with that deep bass voice enunciating every word distinctly.

'Ru-bbish,' the same person growled from some corner. In the darkness a bronze object glinted in a puzzling, dull way, reminding me of a Roman soldier's helmet. I guessed that this was the air vent in the stove.

Subdued voices hummed away in the room and they merged into one dark chaos of fiery words, so that it was impossible to make out who was saying what. Someone on the window-sill above my head asked in a loud, mocking voice: 'Are we going to read or not?'

It was the pale, long-haired young man who said this. Everyone fell silent and all I could hear was the deep voice of the reader. Matches flickered and the little red flames of cigar-ettes lit up faces of people deep in thought, their eyes screwed up or wide open.

The reading continued for a tediously long time and I grew tired of listening, although I liked those sharp provocative words which formed themselves into convincing ideas so simply and easily.

Then suddenly the reader's voice broke off and the room

was filled with cries of protest: 'Renegade!' 'Sounding brass!' 'That's spitting on the blood shed by heroes.' 'And after the execution of Generalov, of Ulyanov . . .'

And once again the young man's voice rang out from the window-sill: 'Gentlemen, is it not possible to substitute abuse with suggestions that are serious and to the point?'

I do not like arguments and I find that I cannot listen to them. For me, it is difficult to follow the capricious mental leaps of over-excited minds and I always find the blatant conceit of people engaged in argument most irritating.

The young man leaned down from the window-sill and asked me: 'You, Peshkov, are a baker, aren't you? I'm Fedoseyev. We must get to know each other. In my opinion one can't achieve anything here, this noise will go on for hours and there's not much point in it. Shall we go?'

I had already heard that Fedoseyev was the organizer of a very serious-minded group of young people and I liked his pale, nervous face with its deep eyes.

As he walked with me across the fields he asked if I had any friends among the workmen, what books I had read and if I got much free time. Among other things he asked me: 'I've heard about this bakery of yours. It's strange that you waste your time on such nonsense. What good is it to you?'

For some time I myself had felt that the place was no use to me and I told him so. He was pleased by what I said and firmly shook my hand. With a bright smile he told me that the following day he was going away for three weeks and that when he returned he would let me know how and where to meet. Business in the bakery was very good, but my own personal life was worse than ever. They had moved to new premises and my round of duties became even wider. I had to work in the bakehouse, take rolls round to people's flats, to the Academy and to the 'Institute for Daughters of the Gentry'. The young girls shoved little notes in my basket as they picked the buns out and I would often read in amazement those cynical words scrawled in almost child-like handwriting on those dainty pieces of fine paper. I felt very awkward when a cheerful crowd of pure, bright-eyed young ladies surrounded my basket and turned over the heap of buns with their tiny pink paws and pulled funny faces. As I watched them I tried to guess which of them had been writing shameless little messages without perhaps even understanding how disgraceful they really were. And as I recalled those filthy 'houses of comfort' I thought: 'Could it be possible that the "invisible thread" stretched from them even to *this* place?'

One of the girls, a brunette with large breasts and thick, plaited hair, stopped me once in the corridor and said in a soft, hurried voice: 'I'll give you ten kopecks if you deliver this note for me.'

Her dark, tender eyes filled with tears as she looked at me and bit her lips hard, while her cheeks and ears turned bright red. I very nobly refused to accept the ten kopecks and I took the note and handed it to a son of one of the members of the law courts – a tall student with the flushed cheeks of a consumptive. He offered me fifty kopecks and silently and thoughtfully counted out the money in small change. When I said that I did not need his money he tried to put the coins back into his trouser pockets, but he missed and the coins scattered over the floor.

He looked on dismayed as the coins rolled in all directions and he rubbed his hands together so hard that the joints cracked. Then he murmured with a deep sigh: 'What shall I do now? Well, goodbye. I must think . . .'

I did not discover what he thought, but I felt very sorry for the young lady. Soon afterwards she disappeared from the Institute and fifteen years later I met her when she was a teacher in a Crimean gymnasium. She was ill with tuberculosis and talked about the whole world with the unremitting spite of someone hurt by life.

When I had finished delivering the rolls I would go to sleep. In the evenings I worked in the bakehouse, so that by midnight the shortening for the pastries was in the shop. The bakehouse was near the town theatre and after the play people would drop in to devour hot puff pastry. Afterwards I would knead the dough for bread that was sold by weight, and for the French rolls. Kneading about 570 or 720 pounds of dough with one's bare hands was no joke. Then I went to sleep again for an hour or two and then started taking the rolls around once more.

And so it went on, day after day.

I had an almost unbearable urge to sow the seeds of what was 'reasonable fine and eternal.' Since I was a sociable person, I was able to give a lively account of what I thought, and my imagination was stimulated by what I had experienced and by what I had read. I needed very little material to turn an everyday fact into an interesting story, with the 'invisible thread' twisting itself about capriciously as its basis. I knew some of the workmen from the Krestovnikov and Alafuzov factories. An old weaver called Nikita Rubtsov was especially close to me. He was a restless, clever man who had worked in almost all the textile factories in Russia.

'I've been wandering round the world for fifty-seven years, my dear Aleksei Maksimych, you young rascal, you bright new shuttle,' he would say in his muffled voice, while his grey, sickly-looking eyes smiled at me through dark lenses which he had joined together himself with a piece of brass wire, leaving green patches of oxide on the bridge of his nose and behind his ears. The weavers called him 'the German' because he shaved his beard, leaving a bristly moustache and a thick clump of grey hair under his lower lip. He was of medium height, broad-chested and was filled with a sombre cheerfulness.

'I love going to the circus,' he said as he leaned his bald, cone-shaped skull on his left shoulder. 'How they train these horses and cattle, eh, what do you think? A comforting thought! I respect cattle and I think to myself. "That means that people should be able to be trained in the same way to use their brains." Circus trainers bribe cattle with sugar. Well, of course, we can buy our own in a shop. But we need sugar for the *soul*, and that sugar is called *kindness*. It means, boy, you should show kindness and not go around with a club as we normally do – am I right?'

He himself was not kind to people and talked to them disdainfully and mockingly. When he was arguing he retorted by way of monosyllabic exclamations in a clear attempt to insult his opponent.

When I first met him he was in a pub, where some men were just about to give him a good beating. One or two blows had already been struck, but I intervened and took him away.

'Did those punches hurt?' I asked as I walked with him in the darkness, through the fine autumn drizzle.

'Well, do *you* think that was a real beating?' he said indifferently. 'Wait a minute, why do you talk to me so formally?'

From this moment we became firm friends. At first he made fun of me wittily and skilfully, but when I told him about the part the 'invisible thread' played in our lives he exclaimed thoughtfully: 'No, you're no fool, oh no!' And he began to treat me in an affectionate, paternal way, even calling me by my first name and patronymic.

'Your ideas, my dear Aleksey Maksimych, are corect, only no one will believe you . . . they're no use to you.'

'*You* believe me, don't you?'

'Me – I'm a stray dog with a short tail. But people are all dogs on a chain and each of them has a lot of burrs sticking to his tail – wives, children, accordions, galoshes. And each dog adores its kennel. They won't believe you. Once we had a real to-do at the Morozov factory! The ones who tried to push in front got it on the forehead. But your forehead is not your arse, and it hurts for a long time afterwards.'

He talked rather differently when he made friends with Shaposhnikov the locksmith who worked at the Krestovnikov factory. The consumptive, Yakov, who played the guitar and was an expert on the Bible, amazed him by his violent denial of God.

77

As he spat gobbets of blood all over the place from his rotten lungs Yakov, with great passion and zeal, tried to prove his point: 'Firstly, I was not created ":in the image and likeness of God". I know nothing, I'm incapable of doing anything and what's more, I'm not a good man – far from it! Secondly, God does not know how hard life is for me. Either he *does* know, and is powerless to help, or he can help but doesn't want to. Thirdly, God is not omniscient, not omnipotent, not merciful. To put it more simply, he just does not exist! It's all a fiction, pure fiction. All of life is a fiction. But you won't fool me!' Rubtsov was struck dumb, then he went grey from anger and started swearing wildly. But Yakov rendered him impotent with his quotations from the Bible, expressed in powerful language, and forced him to keep quiet and huddle up deep in thought.

As he spoke Shaposhnikov looked almost terrifying. His face was swarthy and thin, and he had the curly black hair of a gipsy.

Wolf-like teeth glinted between his blueish lips, and his dark eyes stared motionlessly into his opponent's face. I found that oppressive, crushing stare hard to bear. His eyes reminded me of the megalomaniac. As he walked away with me from Yakov, Rubtsov said gloomily: 'No one has ever attacked God in my presence. I've never heard anything like it. I've heard lots of things in my time, but *nothing* like this. Of course, that man is not long for this world. Well, it's a shame! He got so worked up arguing it made him *white hot*. Interesting, my friend, interesting.' He quickly became firm friends with Yakov and when he spoke he seemed to boil over and became very excited, rubbing his inflamed eyes every now and then with his fingers.

'Ye-es,' he said grinning, 'so God has got the sack. Hm! As far as the Tsar is concerned, my smart lad, I have my own feelings: the Tsar does not stand in my way. But the trouble is not the Tsars – it's the masters. I could make my peace with any Tsar you care to name, even Ivan the Terrible. Yes, sit there and reign if you like, only let me have justice from my master, that's it! If you let me have that I shall chain you to the throne with golden fetters and idolize you . . .'

When he read *King Hunger* he said: 'That's all perfectly correct, of course!' When he first saw a printed pamphlet he asked: 'Who wrote that for you? Very clearly put. You should thank him.' *

Rubtsov had an insatiable appetite for knowledge. He listened to Shaposhnikov's annihilating blasphemies with the closest attention. For hours on end he would listen to my stories about the books I had read. He would laugh with joy, toss back his head – making his Adam's apple stick out – and say rapturously: 'Man's brain is an amazingly clever piece of work!'

He himself had difficulty in reading, as he was handicapped by his bad eye. But he knew a great deal and often astonished me: 'The Germans have a carpenter who is extraordinarily clever – the king himself calls him in for advice.'

When I had questioned him on this point it became clear that he was talking about Bebel.

'How do you know this?' I asked.

'I *know*,' he answered curtly, scratching his round skull with his little finger.

The wearisome chaos of life did not interest Shaposhnikov and he was completely obsessed with denying God's existence and with poking fun at the clergy. He had a particular dislike of monks. Once Rubtsov, in an attempt to make peace, asked him: 'Yakov, why is it only *God* you attack all the time?'

This made him howl even more bitterly: 'Well, what's to prevent me? For almost twenty years I believed and lived in fear of him. I suffered because it was impossible to quarrel, it was all decreed from above, and I lived in chains. When I read the Bible and grasped its meaning I could see that it was all fiction. Yes, fiction, Nikita!'

He waved his arm as though he were trying to snap the 'invisible thread', and he was close to tears.

'I shall die before my time because of all this.'

* Author's note: 'Thank you, Aleksey Nikolayevich Bakh!'

79

I had some other interesting acquaintances as well and I often used to visit old friends in Semyonov's bakery. They were always pleased to see me and listened to me eagerly. But Rubtsov lived in the Admiralty suburb, while Shaposhnikov lived in the Tartar quarter, far beyond the Kaban, about three miles away, and I saw them only rarely. But it was impossible for anyone to come to *me*, as I had nowhere to entertain and besides, the new baker, a retired soldier, was friendly with the gendarmes.

The back of the gendarmerie adjoined our yard and those 'blue coats' would climb over our fence to fetch rolls for Colonel Hanhardt and bread for themselves. Moreover, I was advised not to 'show myself among people', so as not to attract too much attention to the bakery. I could see that my work was beginning to have no meaning for me. More and more often people with no concern for the business took money out of the till so freely that sometimes we did not have enough to pay for the flour.

Derenkov would tug his beard sadly and say: 'We'll go bankrupt in the end.' He had a hard domestic life as well. Nastya, with her red curly hair, would go around pregnant and snort like an evil cat as she looked on everything and everyone with her green, offended eyes. She would march straight at Andrey as though he did not exist, while he would grin guiltily, step out of her way and sigh. Sometimes he used to complain: 'No one takes anything seriously here. Everyone takes what he can, it's so stupid. I bought myself half a dozen socks and they've all disappeared.'

The story about the socks was funny, but I could not bring myself to laugh when I saw that modest man, who had nothing mercenary about him, trying to keep a useful business going, while everyone around him treated it frivolously, recklessly, destroying it.

Derenkov did not expect gratitude from the people he worked for, but he did have a right to a more friendly, considerate attitude – and this he did not get. His family soon fell apart: his father became ill with some form of mild religious mania, while his youngest brother started drinking and going with girls. His sister was like a stranger and was evidently having an unhappy affair with the red-headed student: I often saw her eyes swollen with tears, and this made me hate him.

I thought that I was in love with Marya Derenkova. I was also in love with our shop assistant Nadezhda Shcherbatova, a rather plump red-cheeked girl with a perpetual warm smile on her crimson lips. In general, I was in love with everyone. My age, my temperament and the mess my life was in just asked for a relationship with a woman, and this had come late rather than early.

I needed a woman's affection or at least some kind of friendly relationship with one, as I felt the need to speak frankly about myself, to sort out my muddled, incoherent thoughts and the chaos of what I had lived through. I did not have any real friends. People who looked upon me as 'material for processing' did not awaken any sympathy in me, or encourage sincerity. When I tried speaking about things that did not interest them they would answer: 'Now stop that!'

Then Gury Pletnyov was arrested and taken away to the Kresty prison in St Petersburg.

The first person to tell me the news was Nikiforych, who met me in the street early one morning. As he strode towards me, solemnly and thoughtfully, displaying all his medals, just as though he had just come off parade, he lifted his hand to his cap and passed me by without saying one word. But then he suddenly stopped and spoke right behind me in an angry voice: 'Gury Aleksandrovich was arrested this evening . . .'

And he waved his arm, looked around and then added in a softer voice: 'That young lad's done for!'

I thought that I could see tears shining in his cunning eyes. I knew that Pletnyov had been expecting arrest, had warned me about it beforehand and advised me that neither myself nor Rubtsov (to whom he had become closely attached, like myself) should meet him.

Nikiforych looked down at the ground and asked in a bored voice: 'Why don't you come to see me?'

So that evening I called on him. He had just woken up and was sitting on his bed drinking kvass. His wife was sitting huddled up by the window mending trousers.

'Well, there you are,' the policeman said as he scratched his chest, with its thick growth of hair all over it, just like the fur of a raccoon. He surveyed me thoughtfully and added: 'Yes, he's been arrested. They found a saucepan at his place for heating printing ink for pamphlets against the Tsar.'

He spat on the floor and shouted angrily at his wife: 'Give me my trousers!'

'In a minute,' she answered without raising her head.

'She's sorry for him and keeps on crying,' the old man said as he stared at his wife. 'And I'm sorry as well. However, what can a student do against the Tsar?' He started dressing himself and said: 'I'm just going out for a few minutes . . . Put the samovar on . . .'

His wife looked out of the window without moving, but when he had disappeared behind the door of the hut she quickly turned round, held her tightly clenched fist towards it and said with great venom through her bared teeth: 'Ugh, the old bastard!'

Her face was swollen from crying and her left eye was almost closed by a great bruise. She jumped up, went over to the stove, leaned over the samovar and hissed: 'I'll be unfaithful to him, so much, it'll make him howl like a wolf. Don't you believe him, not a single word he says! He'll trap you. He's always lying and feels sorry for no one. He's been fishing around and knows everything about you. That's what he lives on, that's his kind of sport – catching people.'

She came right up to me and spoke like someone begging: 'Will you be nice to me, then?'

I found her unpleasant but she looked at me with such keen yearning that I embraced her and started stroking her coarse, dishevelled oily hair.

'Who's he watching now?'

'Some people renting rooms in Rybnoryadsky Street.'

'Do you know their names?'

She answered smiling: 'Now I'm going to tell him what you asked me! Here he comes . . . it was *him* who tracked down Gury . . .'

And she jumped over to the stove.

Nikiforych had brought a bottle of vodka, jam and bread. We sat down to drink tea. Marina sat next to me and was particularly friendly, peering into my face with her good eye. Her husband tried to inspire me again. 'This invisible thread is in people's hearts, in their bones. Well, can *you* remove it, and tear it out? The Tsar is God to the people!'

And he asked quite unexpectedly: 'Now you know all about books, have you read the Gospels? Tell me, in your opinion, is it all true what they say there?'

'I don't know.'

'Well, I think there's a lot that's unnecessary there. Lots of it. For example, about beggars. They're called the blessed – what's blessed about them? That's a bit of idle talk. And concerning the poor, there's a lot I just don't understand. You must distinguish the poor man from the impoverished. Poor means bad! And impoverished is unhappy, perhaps. That's the way you should reason, it's best.'

'Why?'

He looked at me inquisitively, fell silent, and then continued in a distinct and rather weighty voice. Obviously, these were ideas that he had examined very carefully.

'There's a lot of compassion in the Gospels, but compassion is harmful. That's what I think. Compassion demands enormous sums of money being spent on unnecessary and even harmful people. Almshouses, prisons, lunatic asylums. Strong, healthy people should be helped, so they do not waste their strength. But we go and help the weak, as if you could make them strong. The crux of the matter is that the strong grow weak and the weak are millstones round their neck. That's what you should worry about! There's a lot of rethinking to be done. You must understand that life turned its back on the Gospels a long time ago and now it goes its own way. Now can you see what ruined Pletnyov? Compassion. We give to the poor and the students perish. Where's the sense in it?'

This was the first time that I had heard these ideas expressed so incisively, although I had come across them before. They are in fact more persistent and widespread than is commonly supposed. Seven years later, when I was reading about Nietzsche I vividly remembered the philosophy of that policeman from Kazan. Moreover, I would add that I rarely found ideas in books which I had not heard about earlier, in real life. And the old 'manhunter' talked on and on, tapping in time to his words on the edge of the tray. His thin-looking face was covered with a deep frown, although he was not looking at me, but at the brightly polished bronze mirror of the samovar.

'It's time you were off,' his wife said. He did not answer, however, but kept stringing one word after the other to the driving piston of his thoughts and suddenly they took a new direction, so that it was impossible for me to grasp them.

'You're no fool and you can read and write. Whatever gave you the idea of being a baker? You could earn just as much in the service of the Tsar . . .' As I listened to him I wondered how I could warn strangers in Rybnoryadsky Street that Nikiforych was following them. Sergey Somov, about whom I had heard a lot of interesting things and who had just returned from exile in Yalutorovsk, had rooms there.

'Clever people should keep together, like bees in a hive or wasps in their nests. The Tsar's empire . . .'

'Just look at the time, nine o'clock,' his wife said.

'Damn!'

Nikiforych stood up and started buttoning his uniform.

'Well, not to worry, I'll take a cab. Good-bye, my friend. Call again – and don't be shy . . .'

As I left the hut I firmly decided never to be Nikiforych's 'guest' again. That old man repelled me, although he *was* interesting.

His words about the harmful effects of compassion troubled me deeply and firmly engraved themselves in my memory. I felt that there was some truth in them but I found it annoying to think that they came from a policeman. Quarrels on this subject were fairly common and one of them particularly tormented me.

A 'Tolstoyan' arrived in the town, one of the first I had ever met. He was a tall muscular man with a swarthy complexion, a black goatee beard and the thick lips of a negro.

He would stoop and look at the ground, but at times he would rapidly jerk his bald head and singe me with the passionate fire of his dark, moist eyes. A certain loathing burned in that piercing stare.

The discussion took place in one of the professor's rooms. There were a lot of young men, including a thin, elegant-looking master of divinity in a black silk gown which very much enhanced his pale handsome face that was lit by the dry smile of his cold grey eyes.

The Tolstoyan talked for a long time about the eternal, unshakeable foundations of the great truths of the Gospel. His voice sounded rather muffled. He spoke in short sentences, but his words were very penetrating and they conveyed a feeling of the truth of sincere faith and he accompanied them by a monotonous movement of his hairy left hand, as though he were hacking away at something, while he kept his right in his pocket.

Next to me, in one corner, I could hear them whispering.

'He's an actor.'

'*Very* theatrical, yes . . .'

Not long before, I had read a book, by Draper, I think, about the struggle of Catholicism against science and it seemed to me that the Tolstoyan who was speaking was one of those frenzied believers in the salvation of the world by love, one of those men who were ready, out of pure compassion for people, to cut them up and burn them on bonfires.

He was dressed in a white broad-sleeved shirt, with some

kind of greyish old smock hanging over it – this also distinguished him from everyone else. At the end of his sermon he shouted: 'Well now, are you on Christ's side or Darwin's?' He seemed to hurl this question as though it were a stone into a corner where young people were sitting huddled together and from which the eyes of young men and girls stared at him in fear and in rapture. His speech had evidently made a great impression on everyone. They were all silent and lowered their heads, deep in thought. He scrutinized everyone with a burning look and added in a stern voice: 'Only Pharisees try to reconcile these two irreconcilable principles and by so doing shamelessly deceive themselves and corrupt others with their lies . . .'

The little priest stood up, neatly threw the sleeves of his gown back and started speaking in a smooth voice, with venomous politeness and a condescending smile.

'You obviously maintain the vulgar opinion about the Pharisees. It is not so much crude as erroneous through and through . . .'

To my extreme astonishment he started demonstrating that the Pharisees were genuine and honest guardians of the testaments of the Jewish people and that they always joined them in the struggle against their enemies.

'For example, read Josephus Flavius.'

The Tolstoyan leaped to his feet, 'struck' Flavius down with a broad devastating sweep of his arm and shouted: 'Even nowadays nations attack their friends with the aid of their own enemies, nations have to act against their will, they're persecuted and coerced. What do I care for your Flavius?'

The priest and some of the others tore the main theme of this argument to shreds and it simply vanished.

'Truth is love,' the Tolstoyan exclaimed and his eyes flashed with hatred and disdain.

I felt intoxicated by all these words and I could not make any sense out of them. The floor seemed to shake underneath me in that whirlpool of words and I often thought despairingly that there was no one on earth so stupid and lacking in talent as myself.

The Tolstoyan wiped the sweat off his purple face and shouted violently: 'Throw the Gospels out, abandon them so you can put an end to your lying! Crucify Christ again – that would be more honourable!'

And the question 'How *is* this?' loomed up before me like a brick wall. If life was an unceasing *struggle* for happiness on earth then compassion and love could only impede its progress.

I learned that the Tolstoyan's name was Klopsky, and I also discovered where he lived. The next day I went to see him. He lived in a house with two spinsters and used to sit with them at a table in the garden, in the shade of an enormous old lime. He was wearing white trousers and the same shirt, unbuttoned over his dark hairy chest. He was tall, angular and had a withered look so that he corresponded exactly to my conception of a homeless apostle preaching the truth.

He scooped up raspberries and milk with a silver spoon, eating with great relish, smacking his thick lips and blowing little white bubbles from his cat-like whiskers after each gulp. One of the spinsters was serving him while the other leaned against the trunk of the lime with her hands on her breast, dreamily gazing at the hot, dusty sky. They were both wearing light, lilac-coloured dresses and were practically indistinguishable from one another.

The Tolstoyan spoke to me warmly and eagerly about the creative power of love, stating how necessary it was to develop this feeling in one's soul, and how this feeling alone was capable of 'linking man with the spirit of the universe!', with the love that was scattered everywhere in life.

'Only love can bind one man to another. Without love life is incomprehensible. Those who say that the law of life is struggle are blind spirits, doomed to perish. Fire cannot be put out by fire – and so evil cannot be overcome by the power of evil!'

But after the women had left, their arms round each other, and when they had disappeared deep in the garden in the direction of the house, this man blinked as they went and asked me: 'And who are *you*?'

When he had heard what I had to say he tapped his fingers on the table and started telling me that a man was a man *anywhere* and that one must strive not to improve one's status in life, but to educate the spirit to love people instead.

'The lower man puts himself, then the nearer he is to the real truth of life, to its most sacred wisdom . . .'

I was rather sceptical of his knowledge of this 'sacred wisdom' but I did not say anything, since I sensed that he found me boring. He looked at me with eyes full of rejection, yawned, put his hands on the back of his neck, stretched his legs out wearily, covered his eyes up and murmured, just as though he were dreaming: 'Obedience to love – that is the law of life.'

Then he shuddered, waved his arms as though he were clutching at something in the air and stared at me with a frightened expression: 'Well, I feel tired now. Good-bye!'

He covered his eyes up once more and clenched his teeth as if they were hurting him. His lower lip dropped and his upper one turned upwards. The bluish hair of his thin whiskers bristled.

I left with a feeling of animosity and with vague doubts as to his sincerity. Early in the morning, a few days later, I delivered some rolls to one of the university lecturers whom I had come to know: he was a bachelor, a drunkard, and once again I met Klopsky. He must have had a sleepless night: his face was brownish, his eyes were red and swollen, and it seemed that he was drunk.

The fat lecturer, who was blind drunk, was sitting on the floor in his underwear with a guitar in his hands amidst a chaos of furniture, beer bottles, and discarded clothes. There he sat, rocking himself and growling: 'Mer-cy . . .'

Klopsky shouted angrily and abruptly: 'There's no such

thing as mercy. We shall either perish from love, or we shall all be crushed in the struggle for it. Either way we're doomed to destruction . . .'

He seized me by the shoulder, led me into the room and said to the lecturer: 'Here he is, ask him what he wants. Ask him if he needs to love people.'

The lecturer looked at me with eyes full of tears and burst out laughing: 'He's the baker! I owe him some money.'

He lurched forward with his hand in his pocket, produced a key and held it out to me: 'Come on, take everything there is!'

But the Tolstoyan seized the key and waved his arm at me: 'Clear off! You'll get your money later!'

Then he flung the rolls which he had taken from me onto a sofa in one corner. He had not recognized me and I was pleased by this. As I left I kept in mind what he had said about perishing from love and I harboured a deep repulsion towards him in my heart.

I was soon told that he had confessed his love to one of the spinsters in the house where he was living and that very same day admitted his love to the other. The sisters shared their joy, which turned into bitterness towards the suitor. They ordered the house porter to tell that 'apostle of love' to clear out of their house at once. He disappeared from the town. The question of the meaning of love and mercy in life is a terrifying and complex one, and I encountered it at an early age, at first in the form of an ill-defined but acute feeling of inner discord. Afterwards it took a precise form, in well-articulated words: 'What is the role of love?' All that I had read was permeated with the ideas of Christianity and humanism, with cries for compassion towards people – the best people I knew at this time spoke about the same things eloquently and passionately. But everything in my immediate surroundings had almost nothing whatsoever to do with compassion for people. Life unfolded itself before me as an endless chain of hostility and cruelty, as an incessant, obscene struggle to possess what was worthless. Personally, I needed only books, and nothing else had any meaning for me.

I needed only to go out into the street and sit for an hour or so by the gates to understand that all those cab-drivers, porters, workmen, clerks, merchants did not live in the same way as myself and that those people whom I had grown to love did not want the same things and were not following the same path. Those people whom I respected and trusted were curiously alien and solitary, and they seemed to be outsiders among the great crowd, among the filthy, cunning toiling of ants laboriously building up the hills of their lives.

This kind of life struck me as thoroughly stupid and deadly boring. And I often noticed that people were compassionate and loving only in what they said, but in their actions they submitted to the general order of things without even noticing it.

Life was now very hard for me.

One day Lavrov the veterinary surgeon, a man with a sallow face swollen with dropsy, told me breathlessly: 'Cruelty must be increased to such an extent that everyone becomes tired of it, repelled by it, just like this damned autumn!'

Autumn had come early, the weather was rainy and cold, and there were many cases of illness and suicide. Lavrov poisoned himself with potassium cyanide, since he had no intention of waiting to be suffocated by dropsy. 'He spent his life healing animals and he died like one!' said Mednikov (a tailor and Lavrov's landlord) as he followed the coffin. He was a pious little man who knew all the prayers of the Holy Virgin by heart. He used to thrash his children (a seven-year-old girl and a boy of eleven who attended the local gymnasium) with a three-thonged strap and then beat his wife on the thighs with a bamboo cane. He would complain: 'The Universal Judge has passed judgment on me for copying this system from a Chinaman, it seems. But I have *never* set eyes on a Chinaman – except in shop-signs and pictures.'

One of his workmen, a dejected looking, bandy-legged man

by the name of 'Dunka's Husband', used to say of his master: 'I'm afraid of meek people who are *religious* as well! You can spot a wild character right away and you always have time to hide. But a meek person will creep up on you unseen, like a crafty snake in the grass and suddenly sting the most precious part of your soul. Meek people frighten me . . .' There was truth in what Dunka's husband said – that meek, cunning old informer and Mednikov's favourite.

Sometimes it seemed that meek people, by eating away at the stony heart of life-like lichen, made it more yielding and fertile. But, more often, when I observed the great number of meek people, with their crafty adaptability to what was vile, with their elusive fickleness, spiritual tractability and gnat-like droning, I felt like a hobbled horse in a swarm of flies.

These were my thoughts as I left the policeman.

The wind sighed and made the street lamps flicker. It seemed that the dark grey sky was trembling as it spread an October rain as fine as dust over the earth. A drenched prostitute was dragging a drunk up the street, holding him under the arms and pushing him as he muttered and sobbed. The woman answered him in a weary, empty voice: 'And that's *your* lot in life . . .'

Yes, I thought to myself, someone is dragging and shoving *me* into nasty corners, showing me filth and sadness, and a strange motley assortment of people. I'm tired of all that.

Perhaps this was not exactly what I was thinking, but this thought nonetheless flared up in my brain and it was precisely on that evening that for the first time, I felt a tiredness of soul, a corrosive mould in my heart. From that moment onwards I began to feel worse, to look upon myself objectively, as it were, and coldly, with the hostile eyes of a stranger. I could see that almost every man harboured, in the same awkward, chaotic way, a host of contradictions, not only in word and deed, but in feeling as well and that this capricious game was particularly oppressive.

And I observed this game being played out within myself,

which was even worse. I felt that I was being pulled in all directions, to women and books, workmen and cheerful students, but I missed the boat every time and I lived neither 'here nor there', spinning round like a top, while some unseen but powerful hand was fiercely lashing me with an invisible whip. When I discovered that Yakov Shaposhnikov was in hospital I tried to visit him, but a fat woman with a crooked mouth, spectacles and a white scarf from under which red limp ears hung down told me in an expressionless voice: 'He's dead.' When she saw that I would not leave and stood there without saying a word, she became angry and shouted: 'Well, anything else?'

I lost my temper as well and said: 'You're a fool.'

'Nikolay, throw him out!'

Nikolay was wiping some sort of copper rods with a rag. He grunted and lashed my back with them. I lifted him up, took him out into the street and sat him in a puddle by the hospital front door. He took this very calmly, and sat there goggling. Then he stood up and said: 'You dog!'

I went into the Derzhavin garden, sat down on a bench by the poet's monument and felt a keen desire to do something evil and nasty, so that crowds of people would throw themselves on me, giving me the right to beat them. Although it was a holiday the garden was completely deserted. There was not a soul to be seen and all I could hear was the sound of the wind driving dirty leaves along and rustling a poster that had partly peeled off.

The cold, transparent blue shadows of dusk thickened over the garden. That enormous bronze statue reared up in front of me. I looked at it and thought how that solitary Yakov had lived in this world and tried with all his might to destroy God and yet he died an ordinary death. There was something very oppressive and insulting in all this. And I thought: But Nikolay is an idiot. He should have given me a fight or called the police to have me arrested.

I went to see Rubtsov who was sitting at the table in his little kennel by a small lamp, darning his waistcoat.

I told him: 'Yakov is dead.'

The old man raised his hand in which he was holding the needle and clearly wanted to cross himself. But all he did was wave his arm. He caught the thread on something and swore obscenely, in a soft voice.

Then he growled: 'Well, if it comes to that, we're all going to die, that's an idiotic habit of ours. Yes, my friend. He went and died. There used to be a coppersmith round here, just like him, he's gone too. It was last Sunday, the gendarmes came for him. I got to know him through Gury. He was a clever coppersmith! But he got mixed up with some students. You've heard how rebellious the students are becoming. Right? Well now, sew this jacket up for me, I can't see a damned thing . . .'

He handed over his rags, together with needle and thread, and put his hands behind his back and started pacing round the room, coughing and grumbling: 'Here and there a little flame will flare up and the devil will blow it out. Then the same old boring life begins all over again. It's an unlucky town. I'm getting out while the steamboats are still running.'

He stopped still, scratched his bald head and asked: 'Well, where will *you* go? I've been everywhere. Yes. Absolutely everywhere and all I've done is wear myself out.' He spat and added: 'Life is a lot of filthy rubbish! I've lived and I've achieved nothing, neither for soul or body . . .'

He fell silent and stood in a corner by the door as though he were listening to something. Then he strode over to me and sat on the edge of the table: 'Let me tell you, my dear Aleksey Maksimych, Yakov wasted that big heart of his on God, all for nothing. Neither God nor the Tsar will be any the better if I renounce them. The important thing is for people to get angry with themselves and reject their own rotten lives. That's what we need! Oh yes, I'm old and I was born too late. I shall soon be stone blind. That's a terrible thing! Finished that jacket? Thanks . . . let's go to the pub for some tea . . .'

On the way he seized me by the shoulder as he stumbled through the darkness and muttered: 'Mark my words, people will lose patience. One day they'll get angry and start destroying everything. They'll turn all their rubbish into dust! They'll lose patience!'

Before we reached the pub we came up against a crowd of sailors besieging a brothel, whose gates were being defended by workmen from the Alafuzov factory. 'There's a fight here every holiday,' Rubtsov said approvingly as he took his spectacles off. When he recognized some of his friends among the defenders he quickly joined in the fight, egging them on: 'Hold on, you from the factory! Crush the frogs. Kill the little tiddlers! Ah-ah!'

It was strange and amusing to see the enthusiasm and dexterity which that clever old man fought with, forcing his way through a mass of sailors, warding off their punches and knocking several over with his shoulder. It was a good-natured, cheerful battle and they fought just for the fun of it, from an excess of energy.

A dark mass of bodies crowded the gates, pressing the factory workers back against them. The planks cracked and vigorous shouts rang out: 'Bash that bald-headed old sparrer.'

Two of them managed to clamber up on the roof and they sang harmoniously and boisterously:

> 'We are not thieves, swindlers or bandits,
> We are sons of the sea, fishermen!'

A policeman blew his whistle, brass buttons shone in the darkness. Mud squelched under foot and singing came from up on the roofs.

> 'We cast our nets along dry banks
> In merchants' houses, barns and storerooms.'

> 'Stop. Never hit a man when he's down!'
> 'Grandpa, hold on to your cheek bone!'

Then Rubtsov, myself and another five men – I could not tell whether friend or foe – were taken away to the police station and a lively song floated after us in the tranquil darkness of an autumn evening:

94

> 'Oh, we caught forty pike,
> And we shall make coats out of them!'

'What wonderful people live along the Volga!' Rubtsov exclaimed rapturously. He kept blowing his nose and spitting. Then he whispered to us: 'Make a run for it, but wait for the right moment. What do you want to go to the police station for?'

I dashed into a side street, with some tall sailor following me, leaped across a fence and then another, and from that night onwards I never set eyes again on that dear, clever Nikita Rubtsov.

Life around me became more and more empty. Student disturbances began – I could not understand their meaning and their motives were not clear. All I could see was a cheerful turmoil in which I could discern no systematic struggle and I thought I would have endured even torture in return for the happy opportunity of studying in a university. If someone had suggested, 'Go and study then, but if you do we'll beat you with sticks on the Nikolaev square every Sunday', then I would most certainly have accepted this condition.

When I went into Semyonov's pretzel shop I discovered that the bakers were preparing to go to the university to beat the students up.

'We'll slosh them with weights,' they said with cheerful malice.

I started arguing and swearing at them, but suddenly I was horrified to find that I had no desire, no words to defend the students.

I remember leaving the cellar feeling as though I had been crippled, with an insuperable, utterly deadly anguish in my heart. When night came I sat on the banks of the Kaban throwing stones into the dark water and repeating three words over and over which I just could not get out of my head: 'What to do?'

From pure boredom I started learning the violin and I scraped away in the shop at night, succeeding in disturbing the nightwatchman and the mice. I loved music and tackled my lessons with great enthusiasm. However, during one of them, my teacher, who played in the town orchestra, opened the till which I had forgotten to lock when I had left the shop for a moment. On my return I found him stuffing his pockets. When he saw me at the door he stretched his neck out, held his dreary shaven face towards me and softly said: 'Well, hit me!'

His lips trembled and curiously oily large tears trickled from his colourless eyes. I wanted to hit him, but to stop myself I sat on the floor with my hands underneath me and ordered him to put the money back. He emptied his pockets and went over towards the door. On the way he stopped and said in an idiotically high-pitched, terrified voice: 'Let me have ten roubles!' I gave him the money, but I did not take any more lessons. In December I decided to commit suicide (I have tried to describe my reasons for this decision in my story 'An incident from the life of Makar') but I did not succeed: the story was very clumsy, unpleasant and devoid of any inner truth. However I must point out its virtues – or so they seemed to me – which lay in the fact that there just was no inner truth in the story.

The facts were correct, but they appeared to have been described by someone else and the story was not about *me*. Apart from any literary value the story may have, I do find something pleasant in it, however, as though I had achieved a victory over myself.

I bought a drummer's revolver at the fair: this was loaded with four bullets and I shot myself in the chest, hoping to hit my heart. But I only succeeded in puncturing a lung. A month later I was once again working in the bakery, feeling very confused and impossibly ashamed at what I had done.

However, this work did not last very long. One evening, towards the end of March, I went into the shop after leaving the bakehouse and I saw Khokhol in the shop-girl's room, sitting on a chair by the window thoughtfully smoking a thick cigarette and watching the clouds of smoke very intently.

'Got a moment?' he said without greeting me.

'I've twenty minutes.'

'Sit down then and let's have a talk.'

As always, he was wearing a very tight-fitting knee length coat made from coarse leather. His fair beard spread over his broad chest and a bristly mass of wiry, close-cropped hair stuck out over his stubborn forehead. He had heavy peasant boots that smelled strongly of tar. 'Well now,' he said in a calm soft voice, 'don't you want to come and live with me? I'm from the village of Krasnovidovo, about thirty miles down the Volga. I've got a shop there and you could help me in my business, it won't take up much of your time. I've some good books and I'll help you study. Well, coming?'

'Yes.'

'Be at the Kurbatov quay on Friday morning at six and ask for the boat from Krasnovidovo – the owner is Vasiliy Pankov. But I'll be there already to meet you. Good-bye!'

As he got up he held out the broad palm of his hand and with the other he took a heavy silver watch from the front of his shirt and said: 'So we only took six minutes! Yes, my Christian name is Mikhailo Antonov and my surname Romas.'

He left without looking round and firmly strode over the ground, easily swinging his heavy body which was moulded like an ancient hero's.

Two days later I set out for Krasnovidovo.

The Volga had only recently become free of ice. Upstream, grey, porous ice floes bobbed up and down as they floated through the muddy water. The boat overtook them and they scraped against the sides shattering into sharp crystal flakes. An upstream wind was blowing, driving the waves onto the shore. The sun was blinding and was reflected in dazzling white rays from the glassy blue sides of the floes.

The boat, which was heavily laden with barrels, sacks, boxes, was now under sail, with young Pankov at the rudder. He was smartly dressed in a waistcoat of tanned sheepskin embroidered in the front with multicoloured lace. His face was calm and his eyes cold. He was a taciturn person and hardly looked like a peasant. At the bows stood Pankov's barge hauler Kukushkin with his legs planted wide apart. He was a scruffy-looking man and wore a tattered coat with a piece of rope as a belt, and a crumpled priest's hat. His face was covered in bruises and scratches. As he pushed the ice floes away with the boathook he cursed contemptuously: 'Get out of it, where d'ye think you're going?'

I sat next to Romas on some boxes under the sail and he quietly told me: 'Peasants don't like me, especially the rich ones! One day you'll know what that's like!'

Kukushkin placed the hook across the sides under his legs, and spoke rapturously as he turned his mutilated face towards us.

'Antonych the priest has a particular dislike for you.'

'That's true,' replied Pankov.

'You're like a bone in that old pockfaced dog's throat!'

'But *I* have friends as well – and they'll be *your* friends,' I heard Khokhol say. It was cold. The March sun did not have much warmth yet. The dark branches of bare trees swayed on the banks, and here and there snow lay in the velvety patches in little crevices and in the shadows of bushes lining the hilly bank. Ice-floes were everywhere on the river, just like a flock of grazing sheep. I felt that I was dreaming.

Kukushkin stuffed some tobacco into his pipe and started philosophizing: 'Well, supposing you are *not* the priest's wife. But it's his duty to love all living creatures, as it is written in the Scriptures.'

'Who beat you up?' Romas asked laughing.

'Well, some sort of shady people – most probably small-time thieves.' Kukushkin replied scornfully. Then he added proudly: 'No, I was once beaten up by some artillery soldiers. I just don't know how I survived.'

'Why did *they* beat you up?' Pankov asked.

'Are you talking about *yesterday*? Or that time with the artillery soldiers?'

'Hm-m – *yesterday*.'

'Well, does anyone know *why* you get beaten up? People are like goats – doesn't take much to make them butt! They think it's their duty to start a fight.'

Romas said: 'I think they beat you up because of that tongue of yours. You're too careless in what you say.'

'Well, okay then! I'm an inquisitive man, asking questions about everything is a habit of mine. I love learning something new.' The bows knocked against an ice floe and there was an evil-sounding noise along the side of the boat. Kukushkin lurched forward and seized the hook, and Pankov told him in a critical voice: 'You watch what you're doing, Stepan.'

'Don't you tell me what to do,' Kukushkin muttered as he fended off the ice floes. 'I can't do my job *and* carry on a conversation at the same time.'

Their quarrels were good-humoured, but Romas told me: 'The land here is worse than in our Ukraine, but the people are better. A very capable lot!'

I listened to him attentively and believed what he was saying. I liked his calmness and his simple, forceful, even speech. I felt that this man knew a lot and that he had his own way of judging people. I was particularly pleased by the fact that he did not ask why I had tried to shoot myself. Anyone else in his place would surely have asked this a long time ago and I was so bored by the question. And in fact it was hard to find an answer. The devil only knows why I decided to shoot myself. Without doubt I would have given Khokhol a long-winded, stupid answer. And, generally speaking, I had no desire to think about it at all. It was so good on the Volga, so free and bright. The boat pulled in close to the shore, with the broad sweep of the river on its left. The water washed over the sandy shore, on the side where the meadows were. One could see how it swelled, splashing and rocking bushes along the banks, while the bright spring torrents noisily poured down into it from shallow gullies and crevices. The sun smiled and the black feathers of yellow-beaked crows, busily cawing as they built their nests, gleamed like steel in its rays, and I was touched to see how, in exposed places, the bright green bristly grass was breaking through the earth towards it. My body was cold, but in my soul I felt a quiet joy and sensed that tender young shoots of bright hope were unfolding there as well. The earth was so pleasant at spring-time. Towards afternoon we reached Krasnovidovo. On a high, sharply sloping hill, stood a church with a light-blue cupola. A row of sturdy, well-built huts stretched down along the ridge and the yellow boards of their roofs and brocade-like straw thatching shone in the sun. It was all so simple and beautiful. How many times I had admired this village as I passed by it on a steamboat! When I started unloading the boat with Kukushkin, Romas passed me some sacks from over the side and told me: 'But you seem very strong!'

And without looking at me he asked: 'Doesn't your chest hurt?'

'Not at all.'

I was very touched by the tactful way he put his question. I was particularly afraid that the peasants might find out about my attempted suicide.

'Yes, you're strong all right, more than the job asks for, I would say.'

Kukushkin rambled on. 'What province are you from, young man? Nizhny-Novgorod? They'll call you a water swigger then. Or they'll say to you: "Can you tell us where the gulls are flying from?"'

A tall, lean, barefooted peasant with a curly beard, a thick clump of reddish hair and wearing a cotton shirt and trousers came slipping and stumbling down the slope of the hill, across the thawing clay which was filled with innumerable silvery rivulets. As he approached the bank he said 'Welcome' in a kind sonorous voice. He looked round, picked up a thick pole, then another and laid them across from the bank to the side of the boat. Then he nimbly leaped into it and started shouting orders: 'Press your feet against the ends of the poles so they don't roll over the side, and take hold of the barrels. Hey you, boy, give us a hand.'

He was as handsome as a painting and evidently very strong. Light blue eyes shone piercingly in his flushed face with its large straight nose.

'You'll catch cold, Izot,' Romas said.

'Who – me? Don't worry.'

We rolled a barrel of kerosene on to the shore. Izot looked me up and down and asked: 'Shop assistant?'

'You try and fight him,' Kukushkin suggested.

'I see they've bashed *your* mug in again.'

'But what can you do with them?'

'Who do you mean?'

'The ones who beat you up!'

'Oh, you!!' Izot said with a sigh and then he turned to Romas. 'The carts won't be long. I saw you a long way off up the river. You made it in good time. Antonych, you can go now and I'll look after things here.' It was obvious that this man was very friendly with Romas and most concerned about him, even inclined to be protective, although Romas was ten years older.

Half an hour later I was sitting in a clean comfortable room in a newly-built hut, the walls still smelling of fresh tar and oakum. A lively, sharp-eyed peasant woman was laying the table for supper. Khokhol was picking some books from a trunk and putting them on a shelf by the stove. 'Your room's in the attic,' he said.

I could see part of the village from there, with a gully opposite our hut, and roofs of bath-houses visible among the bushes. Beyond the gully were gardens and dark fields which gently rolled away towards the blue ridge of the forest on the horizon. A peasant dressed in blue was sitting astride a horse, holding a hatchet in one hand, while he shaded his forehead with the other as he gazed at the Volga down below. A cart creaked, a cow lowed heavily, and an old woman dressed in black from head to foot came through the gates of the hut. As she turned her face towards them she shouted: 'To hell with you!'

Two village boys who had been energetically trying to dam a little stream with stones and mud heard her and rushed away as fast as they could.

The old woman picked up a sliver of wood, spat on it and threw it into the stream. She was wearing men's boots and she kicked the dam in and went down to the river.

What kind of life was in store for me here?

I was called in to supper. Izot was sitting at the lower end of the table with his long legs stretched out. The soles of his feet were purple. He was saying something to Romas, but broke off when he saw me come in.

'What's the matter?' Romas asked gloomily. 'Go on, tell me.'

'Well, it's nothing, I've told you everything. Now, it's all decided. We'll manage on our own. You must carry a pistol, if not, a thick stick. When Barinov's around you can't say too much, he and Kukushkin have tongues like women. Now boy, do you like fishing?'

'No.'

Romas talked of the need to organize the peasants and small market gardeners to save them from the clutches of the big buyers. Izot listened to him attentively and then said: 'If you do that those bloodsuckers will make it impossible to earn a living.'

'We'll see.'

'You mark my words.'

I looked at Izot and thought: yes, Karonin and Zlatov-ratsky must base their stories on this kind of peasant. Had I really got into something serious and would I now be working with people who meant business?

When he had finished eating Izot said: 'Now don't rush into it, Mikhailo Antonych. It's never any good being in too much of a hurry. Take it easy!'

When he had left, Romas said in a pensive voice: 'He's a clever, honest man, but it's a pity he's illiterate. He can hardly read at all. But he's trying very hard to learn, you must help him!'

Right up to evening he tried to teach me the price of goods in the shops. 'I sell cheaper,' he said 'than the other two shopkeepers in the village. Of course, they don't like it. They play dirty tricks on me and are planning to beat me up. I don't live here because I like it, or because business is good. There's other reasons. It's rather like what was going on in your bakery.'

I told him that I had already guessed as much.

'Well then, you must knock sense into people somehow – right?'

The shop was locked up and we went round it with a lamp. Someone was walking along the street, squelching as he cautiously stepped over the mud. He kept stumbling heavily as he climbed the front steps.

'Did you hear that? Someone's there! That's Migun, he's a lone wolf, an evil man. He loves doing wicked things, just like a pretty girl flirting. Be careful what you say to him – in fact to *anyone*!'

Afterwards, when we were back in the hut, he lit his pipe, leaned with his broad shoulders against the stove and screwed his eyes up, puffing little streams of smoke into his beard. Then he told me slowly in simple, clear words, that he had noticed a long time ago that I was wasting the years of my youth.

'You're an able boy, stubborn by nature and plainly well-intentioned. But you must study, but not so that books hide real people from you. One old man, a member of some religious sect or other, was so right when he said: "All learning comes from man." People teach more painfully than books and they teach crudely. But what you learn takes firmer roots.'

He told me what I already knew, that, first and foremost, the minds of villagers must be stirred into life. But in these familiar words I could detect a deeper and new meaning.

'Those students of yours babble away about love of the

people, but I say to them: it's impossible to love the people. These are only words ... *love of the people* ...'

He laughed into his beard, looking at me inquisitively. Then he started pacing up and down the room and continued in a firm, persuasive voice: 'Loving means agreeing, condescending, not seeing, forgiving. That's how you should approach women. But how can you fail to see the ignorance of the people, agree with their errors, accept all the vile things they do, forgive their savagery? *Can* we?'

'No.'

'Well, so there! Your friends in the city read and recite Nekrasov all the time, but you won't get far with Nekrasov! You must encourage a peasant with words like these: "Brother, although you're not bad in yourself, you live badly and you have no idea how to improve your life and make it easier. A wild animal, for example, looks after itself better than you and it's better at self-defence. But from you, the peasants, everything came – the nobility, clergy, scholars, tsars – they were *all* peasants once. Now do you see? Understand? Well then, just learn to live so you're not trodden on." '

He went into the kitchen and told the cook to heat the samovar. Then he started showing me his books, almost all of them scientific – Buckle, Lyell, Lecky, Lubbock, Taylor, Mill, Spencer, Darwin. Among Russian authors were Pisarev, Dobrolyubov, Chernyshevsky, Pushkin, Goncharov's '*Frigate Pallas*', Nekrasov. He stroked them with the flat of his palm, affectionately, as though they were kittens and then he growled in a way that was almost touching: 'Good books! This one is very rare, it was ordered to be burnt by the censors. If you want to know what the State really is then read it!' He handed me Hobbes's *Leviathan*.

'This one's also about the State, but it's easier, more cheerful!'

The cheerful book turned out to be Machiavelli's *The Prince*.

While we were having tea he briefly told me about himself. He was the son of a blacksmith from Chernigov. When he was working as a train-greaser at Kiev station he became friendly with some revolutionaries and organized a workers' study group. He was arrested and was in prison for two years. Afterwards he was exiled to Yakutsk for ten years.

'At first I lived with the Yakuts, on a settlement, and I thought I was done for. The winter was so hellish that a man's brain froze. And there was no place for brains there anyway. Then I saw that there were a few Russians there – not many, but Russians all the same! And so they wouldn't get bored the authorities kept sending new ones to join them. They were good people. There was a student by the name of Vladimir Korolenko – he's just come back like me. I got on well with him and then we drifted apart. We were alike in many ways, but friendship doesn't thrive on similarities. He was a serious, stubborn man, capable of any work. He could even paint ikons, and I didn't like this. They say that now he's writing good articles for newspapers.'

He talked for a long time, right up to midnight, and he obviously wanted to be firm friends with me straight away. This was the first time I had such a serious friendship with a man. After my attempt at suicide, I had fallen greatly in my own estimation – I felt like a nobody, guilty in someone's eyes, and I was ashamed to be alive. Romas must have understood this and in a simple, humane way opened the door of his life to me, and put me on the right track.

It was an unforgettable day. After Mass on Sunday we opened the shop and immediately peasants started gathering by the front steps. The first was Matvey Barinov, a filthy, dishevelled man with the long arms of a monkey and with a vacant look in his fine womanish eyes.

'What's the news from the town?' he asked after greeting us. Without waiting for an answer he shouted at the approaching Kukushkin: 'Stepan! Your cats have gobbled up a cockerel again!'

And right away he started telling us how the Governor had left Kazan for St Petersburg to see the Tsar and made him order all the Tartars to be moved to the Caucasus and Turkestan. He praised the Governor: 'A clever man, knows his job . . .'

'You've made it all up,' Romas remarked calmly.

'Me? When?'

'I don't know . . .'

'Really, you never believe what people say, Antonych,' Barinov said reproachfully, and shook his head regretfully. 'But I feel sorry for the Tartars. The Caucasus needs getting used to!'

A small, thin young man came up. He was wearing a ragged coat that had once belonged to someone else. His grey face was distorted by a nervous tic and had twisted his dark lips into a sickly smile. His sharp left eye blinked incessantly and above it twitched a grey eyebrow, mutilated with scars.

'Here's to Migun!' Barinov said mockingly. 'What did you steal last night?'

'Your money,' Migun answered in his sonorous tenor voice as he doffed his hat to Romas.

Pankov, our neighbour, and the owner of our hut came in from the yard wearing a jacket, a red kerchief round his neck and rubber galoshes. A silver chain as long as horses' reins hung over his chest. He weighed up Migun with an angry stare and said: 'You old devil, if you climb into my kitchen garden once more I'll beat your legs with a stick.'

'That's how they talk round here,' Migun calmly observed. He sighed and added: 'But what's life without a fight?'

Pankov started swearing at him but Migun went on: 'What do you mean, *old*? I'm forty six . . .'

'But at Christmas you were fifty-three,' Barinov exclaimed. 'You said this yourself. Why do you have to lie?'

A bearded dignified-looking old man called Suslov* joined us, together with Izot the fisherman, which made ten

---

*I am not good at remembering peasants' names and I have probably mixed them up or distorted them (Gorky's note).

altogether. Khokhol sat on the steps in front of the shop smoking a pipe and silently listening to the peasants. They sat down on the steps and on little benches on either side. It was a cold, colourful day. Clouds swiftly sailed over the blue sky which was frozen by winter. Patches of light and shade seemed to be bathing in rivulets and puddles, at times blinding the eye with their glare, at others caressing in their velvety softness. Smartly-dressed girls glided like peacocks down the street towards the Volga, lifting their skirts as they stepped over puddles and revealing their shoes which seemed to be made of cast iron. Street urchins ran around with crudely made fishing rods on their shoulders and respectable-looking peasants went past, looking at the gathering outside our shop out of the corner of their eye, silently raising their caps and felt hats. Without quarrelling, Migun and Kukushkin tried to sort out that vague question, who could hit harder, the merchant or the landed gentleman?

Kukushkin tried to prove that it was the merchant, while Migun was on the side of the landed gentleman, and his sonorous little tenor voice gained the upper hand over Kukushkin's confused arguments.

'Mr Fingerov's father pulled Napoleon by the beard. And Mr Fingerov would grab two men by their sheepskin collars and knock their heads together and that was that! They would lie there motionless.'

'And so would you,' agreed Kukushkin, but he added: 'Well, a gentleman eats more than a merchant!'

The fine-looking old Suslov sat on the top step and complained: 'Peasants are becoming weak, Mikhailo Antonov. Under gentlemen you were not allowed to do nothing, everyone had some sort of job.'

'Then you'd better sign a petition to have serfdom brought back,' Izot retorted. Romas silently glanced at him and started knocking his pipe out on the railings.

I waited for him to open his thoughts to me. And as I listened attentively to the peasants' disjointed conversation

I tried to imagine exactly what Khokhol would say. It appeared that he had wasted countless opportunities of joining in, but all he did was keep an indifferent silence, sitting there as still as an idol, watching the wind ruffle the water in the puddles and drive the clouds into a thick grey mass. A steamship whistled on the river and down below I could hear the shrill songs of girls, accompanied by an accordion. A drunk strode down the street hiccoughing and growling. He waved his arms about, his legs were strangely bent, and he kept stumbling into puddles. The peasants spoke even slower, their words were filled with dejection and I too felt a gentle sadness, since the cold sky threatened rain and I recalled the incessant noise of the town with its great variety of sounds, the swift movement of people along the streets, their lively speech and the many stimulating words they used. In the evening, during tea, I asked Khokhol when he spoke to the peasants.

'About what?' he replied.

'Aha,' he added, paying great attention to what I said. 'Well, you see, if I talked to them about such things – and in the street as well – I would be sent straight off to live with the Yakuts again.'

He stuffed some tobacco into his pipe, puffed deeply and was immediately enveloped in a cloud of smoke. He calmly told me, in a way I found difficult to forget, that peasants were cautious, distrustful people.

'The peasant is afraid of himself, of his neighbour and particularly of any stranger. It is hardly thirty years since they have been given their freedom and every serf forty years old was born a slave and does not forget it. Freedom is something difficult to understand. To put it simply, freedom is living as you like. But the authorities are everywhere and stop you living as you like. The Tsar took the serfs away from the landlords, therefore the Tsar alone must be lord over all the peasants. And to return to what I was saying – what *is* freedom? Suddenly the day will come when the Tsar will announce what it means. A peasant has a deep faith in the Tsar, the sole lord of all land and wealth. He took the peasants away from their owners, in the same way he can take steamships and shops away from merchants. Peasants are *for* the Tsar, because they understand how bad it is to have a lot of masters and that *one* is better. The peasant is only waiting for the day when the Tsar will teach him the meaning of his freedom. Then everyone will grab what he can. Everyone wants this day to come, and yet everyone is afraid, everyone is living on tenterhooks lest he misses that decisive day of redistribution. And he is afraid of himself. He wants a lot, there's a lot for the taking, but how to get it? They are all after one and the same thing. What's more, everywhere there's so many officials you just can't count them and they are hostile to peasants and to the Tsar as well. But life is impossible without the authorities, without them everyone would fight and kill each other.'

The wind angrily lashed the windows, bearing the full flood of spring rain. A grey mist drifted down the streets and deep in my heart I felt grey as well, and depressed. A calm, soft, thoughtful voice said: 'You must teach a peasant to try and gradually wrest the Tsar's power away from him and take it into his own hands. You must tell him that the people should have the right to choose their government from among themselves – policemen, governors and tsars as well . . .'

'That would take a hundred years,' I said.

'Did you expect to get it all done by Whitsun?' Khokhol asked seriously. In the evening he went off somewhere, and at eleven o'clock I heard a shot in the street, quite near me. I jumped out into the pouring rain and saw Mikhail Antonich going towards the gates – a huge black figure carefully and unhurriedly avoiding the streams of water.

'Well, what do you want? *I* fired the shot.'

'At whom?'

'Some men with sticks attacked me. I told them: "If you

don't clear off I'll fire." They didn't listen. Well, I fired into the sky – you can't hurt that!'

He stood in the hall and snorted like a horse as he took off his clothes and wrung the water out of his beard.

'Those damned shoes are no good, I shall have to change them. Can you clean a revolver? Please do it for me, before it goes rusty. Smear it with kerosene.'

His imperturbable calm and the gentle obstinacy in his grey eyes delighted me. When we went inside he stopped in front of the mirror to comb his beard and warned me: 'You must be more careful when you go round the village, especially when there's a holiday, or in the evening. Someone might beat *you* up as well. But don't take a stick. This only provokes anyone wanting to pick a quarrel and might make him think you're afraid. But there's nothing to be afraid of. They're cowards themselves . . .'

I now began to lead a very good life and each day brought something new and significant. I started hungrily reading books on the natural sciences and Romas would instruct me: 'You must learn *this* above everything else, Maksimych. The best thoughts of mankind are in science.'

Three evenings a week Izot called on me and I taught him to read and write. At first he was distrustful and his attitude was gently mocking. But after a few lessons he said amiably: 'You explain things very well. You should be a teacher!' And he suddenly suggested: 'You seem to be strong, let's have a go with the stick.'

We took one from the kitchen, sat on the floor, pressed the soles of our feet against each other's and for a long time we tried to lever each other up from the floor. Khokhol grinned and egged us on: 'Well, come on then!'

Finally Izot succeeded in lifting me up and this seemed to make him more favourably disposed towards me.

'Don't worry, you're healthy,' he said, trying to console me. 'It's a pity you can't fish, you could have come with me on the Volga. It's sheer heaven on the river at night . . .'

He was a very enthusiastic and fairly good pupil and would be absolutely amazed at his own progress. Sometimes, during a lesson, he would suddenly get up, take a book from the shelf, raise his eyebrows high and read two or three lines after a great effort. His face would turn red and he would look at me and say in an astonished voice: 'You see, I can read, ever hear anything like it!' Then he would close his eyes and repeat some poetry:

'Just like a mother mourning over the grave of her son,
   So wails the sandpiper over the desolate plain . . .'

'Read it?'

Several times he would ask cautiously, almost in a whisper: 'Tell me, my friend, how it all comes about. A man looks at these commas and hyphens and they turn into words and I recognize them, they're our living words! How do I know this? No one's whispering them into my ear. If these were pictures, then I could understand. But here it seems that the thoughts themselves are printed on the page – how do they do it?'

What could I answer? My 'don't know' annoyed him.

'The work of a magician!' he said sighing, as he peered at the pages and held them up to the light.

There was a pleasing, touching naivety about this man, something transparent and child-like. He came to resemble more and more those wonderful peasants whom I had read about in books. Like all fishermen he was a poet, loved the Volga, quiet nights, solitude, the contemplative life.

He would look up at the stars and ask: 'Khokhol says that some sort of people might be living up there. Do you think that's true? We could send them a signal and ask what their lives are like. I'm sure they're better and more cheerful than ours . . .'

In actual fact he was content with his life. He was an orphan, a lone wolf and he depended on no one in his quiet, beloved fisherman's work. But he was hostile to peasants and warned me: 'Don't you think they're being friendly. They're a cunning lot, deceitful, don't trust them! One moment they're on your side and the next it's completely different. They can only see what suits *them*, and think that anything for the common good is a kind of forced labour.'

And he would talk about the 'Bloodsuckers' with a hatred strange for a man with such a gentle soul.

'Why are they richer than anyone else? Because they are cleverer. Now, you scum, if you're clever, remember: peasants should live in a herd together, as friends, and then they are strong! But now they are splitting the villages up, just like logs into kindling wood. They are their own enemies, a lot of rogues. Just see the trouble Khokhol has with them!'

He was handsome and strong, and very attractive to women, who seemed to possess him.

'Of course, I'm spoiled by them,' he confessed good-naturedly. 'But it's insulting for the husbands, I would feel the same in their place. But you can't help feeling sorry for women, they're like your second soul. They have no holidays get no affection, work like horses and that's all. The husbands have no time for love, but I'm a free man. Many of these wives, in the first year of marriage, feel the taste of their husbands' fists. Yes, I'm to blame here, I play around with them. But there's only one thing I ask: "Women, don't get angry with one another, I can look after all of you! Don't envy one another, you're all alike as far as *I'm* concerned, I'm sorry for you all . . ."'

He smiled in embarrassment and then told me a story: 'Once I very nearly sinned with a real lady, she'd come from the city to her country house. She was a real beauty, white as milk and her hair was like flax. She had little blue kind eyes. I used to sell her fish and I couldn't keep my eyes off her. She would ask: "Why are you looking like that?" and I replied: "You know very well." So she said: "All right then, I'll come to your room tonight, so wait for me." And she kept her word. She turned up. However, she was afraid of mosquitoes, they liked biting her, so nothing happened. "I can't," she said, "they bite terribly." And she was near to tears. A day later her husband turned up, he was some sort of judge. Yes, that's what ladies are like.'

He said this sadly and reproachfully, and added: 'They let *mosquitoes* ruin their lives.'

Izot spoke about Kukushkin in the highest terms: 'Yes, watch him carefully, he has a good soul. He's not liked, though, but they're wrong. He's a chatterer, but everyone's different . . .'

Kukushkin had no land and he was married to a drunken farm labourer, a small woman, but very agile, strong and evil-tempered. He let their hut to the blacksmith, while he himself lived in the bath-house and worked for Pankov. He had a passion for news and if there wasn't any available he would make up different stories himself. They invariably followed the same pattern: 'Have you heard, Mikhailo Antonov? The village constable in Tinkov is going into a monastery and quitting his job. Says he doesn't want to fleece the peasants any more. He's had enough!'

Khokhol said seriously: 'If you go on like that you'll be losing all your officials.'

Kukushkin picked bits of hay, straw and chicken feathers out of his uncombed blond hair and said: '*All* of them wouldn't run away. But those with a conscience find it hard to carry out their duties. I can see you don't believe in conscience, Antonych, but you can't get by without it, no matter how clever you are! Listen to this as an example . . .'

And he would start telling me a story about some 'very clever' woman landowner.

'She was such an evil woman that even the Governor, in spite of his very important duties, was obliged to come and visit her. "My lady," he would say, "be more careful in future, just in case. I've heard that rumours about the evil, vile things you do have got as far as St Petersburg."'

'Of course, she gave him a drink and said: "Go in peace,

I can't change my nature!" Three years and a month passed, and then she suddenly called in all her peasants. "Here is my land, take it all and – goodbye. Forgive me, but I must go . . ."'

Khokhol prompted him with the words '. . . into a convent.' Kukushkin looked at him attentively and confirmed what Khokhol had just said: 'Yes, she became a Mother Superior! Have you heard about her?'

'Never.'

'Then how do you know?'

'I know *you*.'

The dreamer shook his head and mumbled: 'Never seen such a distrustful man as you!'

And it was always the same: the wicked, evil people in his stories got tired of doing evil and would disappear without trace. But more often Kukushkin would pack them off to a monastery, like rubbish to a scrap heap. Quite unexpected and weird thoughts would come into his head and he would suddenly frown and declare: 'It was a waste of time defeating the Tartars – they're better than us!'

But Tartars were not at all topical then – people were talking about organizing a fruit-growers' cooperative.

Then Romas would start telling stories about Siberia, about the rich Siberian peasants and Khokhol would mumble thoughtfully: 'If no one fished for herrings for two or three years they would multiply so fast and grow so big the sea would overflow its shores and everyone would be drowned. It's an amazing breeder!'

All the people in the village thought there was not much to Kukushkin, but his stories and strange ideas annoyed the peasants and made them swear and jeer. But they always listened to him with great interest, very attentively, as though there might be some truth in his fantasies. He was called 'Windbag' by respectable people and only Pankov, who was a bit of a show-off, would say seriously: 'There's something mysterious about Stepan.' Kukushkin was a very able worker and could do the job of a cooper or a stove builder, knew all about bees, taught peasant women to breed birds, and he was a skilful carpenter. He was successful in all he did, although he worked slowly, reluctantly. He loved cats and about ten well-fed male and female members of the species lived with him in the bath-house, and he fed them on crows and jackdaws. In fact, he taught the cats to eat birds as part of their diet and in this only increased the villagers' dislike of him. His cats smothered chickens and hens. The peasant women in turn hunted Stepan's cats and beat them mercilessly. One could often hear the furious women screaming wildly, but this did not worry him.

'You fools. Cats are hunters, they're more cunning than a dog. When I've taught them to hunt birds we'll breed hundreds of cats. Then we'll sell them and make a profit, you fools!'

He could read and write once but now he had forgotten and he had no desire to refresh his memory. Clever by nature, he was quicker than anyone at understanding the essential meaning of Khokhol's stories.

'Yes, yes,' he would say, frowning like a child swallowing bitter medicine, 'that means Ivan the Terrible never harmed small nations.'

Together with Izot and Pankov, he would come to visit us in the evenings and they would often sit up until midnight listening to Khokhol's stories about the creation of the world, about life in foreign countries, about revolutionary upheavals. He liked the French revolution.

'Now, that was a real turning-point,' he said approvingly. Two years before, he had left his father, a rich peasant with an enormous throat and terrifying bulging eyes. He had married an orphan 'for love', a niece of Izot's, and although he treated her strictly, he let her dress like the women in the town. The father cursed him for his obstinacy and whenever he went past his son's new hut he would spit furiously on it. Pankov let the hut to Romas and built a shop onto it, against the wishes of the rich people in the village. They hated him for it but he gave the appearance of being indifferent towards them. In turn, he spoke contemptuously about them and rudely mocked them when he was in their company.

He found village life oppressive: 'If I knew a trade I would live in the town.'

He was well-built, always immaculately dressed and bore himself like a respectable and very proud citizen. He had a cautious, distrustful mind.

'Did you take on that job because your heart told you, or your head?' he would ask Romas.

'Well, what do *you* think?'

'I don't know. You tell me.'

'In your opinion – what's better?'

'I don't know. And in *your* opinion?'

Khokhol was obstinate and in the end forced the peasant to speak his thoughts: 'The best things come from the *mind*, of course! The mind can't live without profit. And where there's something to be gained, you have something that will last. The heart gives bad advice. If I had followed my heart, then there would have been trouble! I would have set fire to the priest, to stop him poking his nose in where he shouldn't!'

The priest, an evil old man, with a snout like a mole's, had really got Pankov's back up when he interfered in his quarrel with his father. At first Pankov was unfriendly towards me, almost hostile. He even shouted at me as though he were the master. But this soon disappeared. Nevertheless I felt that the hidden distrust of me remained. And I too found Pankov unpleasant.

I remember particularly vividly those evenings in that tiny clean little room with its log walls. The windows were firmly shuttered. A lamp burned on the table in the corner and in front of it stood a smoothly shaven man with a prominent forehead and a large beard. He was saying: 'The meaning of life is that man should move further and further away from beasts.' The three peasants listened to him attentively. All of them had fine, clever eyes. Izot always sat motionlessly, as though he were listening to something far away, something he alone could hear.

Kukushkin kept fidgeting about as though mosquitoes were biting him, while Pankov kept tugging his bright whiskers and quietly pondered: 'So people had to be divided into classes after all.'

I was very pleased that Pankov never spoke rudely to Kukushkin, who laboured on his farm, and he always listened very attentively to the amusing fantasies of this dreamer.

The conversation would come to an end and I would retire to my attic and sit there by the open window looking at the sleeping village and the fields, where an indestructible silence reigned. The night mist was permeated with the light of the stars: the nearer they were to the earth the further away from me they seemed. The utter silence would make my heart sink and my thoughts would flow out into the limitless space where I could see thousands of villages which, like mine, huddled close to the flat earth in complete silence.

Nothing moved, all was silent. I felt that I was being embraced by the warmth of that misty emptiness and it seemed to cling to my heart like thousands of invisible leeches. Gradually I began to feel weak from sleepiness and I was disturbed by a vague uneasiness for which I could find no explanation. I was so small and insignificant in this world . . .

And before me village life loomed up in all its joylessness. Time and again I had heard and read that people in the country lived more healthy, sincere lives than those in towns. But all I could see were peasants engaged in an incessant toil which was almost prison-like. Among them were many sick people, broken by hard work, and there were hardly any cheerful ones. Artisans and workers in the city, who worked just as hard, lived a gayer life and did not complain in such a

117

tiresome and tedious way as those miserable people. A peasant's life did not appear simple to me and it required the utmost care for the soil and a high degree of subtle cunning in relationships with others. There was nothing warm about this poor life, devoid of all thought, and I could see that all the people in the village lived a groping kind of existence, as though they were blind, and that they were all afraid of something, and did not trust each other; and they all had something of the wolf in them.

I found it difficult to understand why they persisted in their hatred of Khokhol, Pankov and all of 'us' who wanted to lead a reasonable life. I could clearly see the advantages of living in the city, with its thirst for happiness, its bold curiosity of mind, the great variety of its aims and tasks. And always, on such nights as these, I remembered two city dwellers and their shop sign: 'F. Kalugin and Z. Nebei, Watchmakers. We also repair different kinds of apparatus, surgical instruments, sewing machines and musical boxes of any make, etc.'

This sign was placed over a narrow doorway in a little shop. On both sides of the door there were dusty windows and F. Kalugin would be sitting at one of them. He had a bump on his bald, yellow skull and wore a magnifying glass in one eye. He was thick-set, round-faced and he hardly ever stopped smiling as he probed at the works of a watch with a pair of fine tweezers or sang some song with his round mouth wide open, partly hidden under his grey bristling moustache. Z. Nebei sat at the other window. He had curly hair, was swarthy looking, with a large crooked nose, eyes as large as plums and a little pointed beard. He was thin and withered, which made him look like a devil. Like Kalugin, he was always taking something to pieces and repairing some small object. From time to time he would unexpectedly shout in his deep voice: 'Tra – ra tam, tam!'

Behind them was a chaotic pile of boxes, machines, wheels of some sort, musical boxes and globes. The shelves were filled with metal objects of all kinds, and the pendulums of numerous clocks swung to and fro on the walls. I could have stayed there the whole day looking at these men working, but my long body shut out the light, which made them stare at me with terrifying faces, waving their arms for me to clear off. As I left I thought enviously: What happiness, to be able to do *everything*!

I respected these men and believed that they knew all the secrets of every machine and instrument, and that they could repair anything in the world. They were *real* people! But I did not like the country and I could not understand the peasants. The women, in particular, were always complaining of illness and they always had 'rumbling in the heart', 'heaviness in the chest', 'gripe in the belly' and they would speak about these symptoms more eagerly than anything else as they sat in their huts, or on the banks of the Volga during holidays.

They were all terribly irritable and swore violently at each other. Just because of a broken earthenware pot, worth about twelve kopecks, three families fought with sticks, an old woman's arm got broken and a young boy had his skull cracked ... Quarrels like these happened every week.

The boys treated the girls with a blatant cynicism and played all kinds of dirty tricks on them. They would catch them out in the fields, lift their skirts up and tie the hems tight with a piece of bast right up over their heads. This was known as 'turning a girl into a flower' and the girls, naked below the waist, would scream and swear, but apparently they found this sport pleasant and untied their skirts afterwards, noticeably slower than they could have. During the late Mass the boys would pinch their bottoms and it seemed that this was their sole reason for going to church. On Sundays the priest would say from his pulpit: 'Cattle! Can't you find another place for your disgraceful carryings-on?'

'Now the Ukrainians, for example, are more poetical in their religion,' Romas would say, 'but here, under the pretext of faith in God, all I see is the crudest instincts of fear and greed. The people here do not possess a sincere love of God, or take any delight in his beauty and strength. Perhaps that's a good thing: in this way they will free themselves more easily from religion. It's a most harmful prejudice, I'm telling you!'

The village boys were boastful, but they were cowards. Three times already they had lain in wait and tried to beat me up in the street at night, but they did not succeed and all I once got was a bang on the leg with a stick. Of course, I did not talk to Romas about these skirmishes, but when he noticed that I was limping he guessed what had happened.

'Hm, so you got a present after all! Didn't I tell you?'

Although he advised me not to go walking at night, I used to go down to the banks of the Volga, over kitchen gardens, and sit there under the willows, peering across the river through the transparent veil of the night, towards the meadows. The Volga flowed with a slow majesty and its waters were richly gilded by the rays of an invisible sun, reflected from a dead moon.

I do not like the moon, there is something sinister about it. It makes me feel sad, and fills me with a desire to howl mournfully like a dog. I was very pleased when I discovered that it did not shine with its own light, that it was dead, and that there could be no life on it. Before, I had imagined it inhabited by bronze people, shaped like triangles, who moved with legs like pairs of compasses, clanging away like Lenten bells. Everything on the moon was made of bronze, the vegetation, animals – everything made an incessant muffled, jangling noise that spelled hostility towards the earth, and told of some evil plot that was being hatched. It was pleasant to discover that it was merely one deserted spot in the heavens. All the same, I wanted a great meteor to fall on the moon with such force it would burst into flames and spread a new light of its own all over the earth. As I watched the slow current of the Volga rock that velvet patch of moonlight, a current that was born somewhere far away in the darkness and which disappeared in the black shadows of the hilly bank, I felt that my mind was becoming more daring and perceptive. Without any effort at all I thought of something that just could not be expressed in words, something that had nothing to do with all the events of the day. The majestic motion of that watery mass was almost soundless.

Along the dark wide waterway a steamboat glided like a monstrous bird with fiery feathers and it left soft sounds in its wake like the beating of heavy wings. A tiny light floated near the meadow bank and it cast a sharp red ray over the water – this was a fisherman spearing fish by torchlight. It was easy to imagine that one of heaven's stars had fallen into the river and was floating in the water like a fiery flower.

All that I had read in books grew into strange fantasies and my imagination perpetually wove pictures of incomparable beauty – I seemed to be drifting in the soft night air down the river. Izot would find me there and at night he looked even bigger and more pleasant.

'You here again?' he would ask, as he sat beside me. For a long time he would not say a word and he gazed at the river and sky in deep silence, stroking the fine silk of his golden beard. Then he would start day dreaming again: 'I'm going to study and learn to read lots of books. Then I'll go down to the river and understand everything! I'll teach other people! Yes. It's a good thing sharing your soul with another man. Even women – a few of them will understand if you speak to them from your heart. Not so long ago a woman was sitting in my boat and she asked: "What will happen to us when we die? I don't believe in hell, or in heaven." How do you like that my friend? They're also . . .' Unable to find the right word he fell silent and finally added: 'Living souls.' Izot was a man of the night. He had a keen feeling for beauty and described it very well in the soft words of a dreaming child. He had a fearless belief in God, although he followed the orthodox teachings of the church, and he pictured God as a large, handsome old man, the kindly, clever master of the universe who could not conquer evil only because: 'He cannot be everywhere at once, too many men have been born for that. But he *will* succeed, you see. But I can't understand Christ at all! He serves no purpose as far as I'm concerned. There is God and that's enough. But now there's another! The son, they say. So what if he's God's son. God isn't dead, not that I know of.'

But most often Izot would sit silently thinking about something and only now and again said with a sigh: 'Yes, that's how things are.'

'What?'

'Oh, I was just talking to myself.'

And once again he would sigh as he peered into the murky distance.

'This life is a good thing!'

I would agree: 'Yes, very good!'

The velvet strip of dark water flowed powerfully past and the silvery regions of the Milky Way arched over it. Huge stars shone like golden larks and one's heart softly sang out its foolish thoughts about the mysteries of life. High over the meadows the sun's rays broke through the reddish clouds and suddenly it spread its peacock's tail over the sky.

'What a wonderful thing – the sun!' Izot muttered with a happy smile. The apple trees were in blossom and the village was buried in pinkish snowdrifts and filled with a bitter smell which spread everywhere, drowning the smells of tar and dung.

Hundreds of flowering trees, festively dressed in a pinkish satin of petals, stretched in even rows away from the village, into the fields. On moonlit nights, when there was a slight breeze, the flowers trembled like moths, made a barely audible rustling sound and it seemed that the village was being submerged in heavy golden-blue waves. Nightingales sang passionately and incessantly, while starlings sang their fervent, tantalizing songs by day and invisible skylarks poured their sweet unending song onto the earth.

During the evenings, when there was a holiday, young girls and married women walked down the street singing songs with their mouths wide open like fledglings and they smiled languidly and drunkenly. Izot smiled as well, just as though he were drunk. He looked thinner, his eyes had sunk into dark pits, his face was even sterner, more handsome and saintly. He would sleep all day long, appearing in the streets only towards evening, looking worried and pensive. Kukushkin mocked him crudely, but affectionately, while Izot grinned in embarrassment and said: 'Be quiet. What can you do?' And he exclaimed rapturously: 'Oh, life is so sweet! How loving life can be, what words there are for soothing the heart! You'll never forget some of them until your dying day. And when you're resurrected they'll be the first thing you remember!'

'Watch out, the husbands will beat you up one of these days,' Khokhol tenderly warned him.

'And they'd have good reason,' agreed Izot.

Almost every night one could hear the high-pitched, moving voice of Migun, which mingled with the sounds of the nightingale and poured out over the gardens, the fields and the river bank. Migun sang fine songs marvellously well, and even the peasants forgave him many crimes because of them. On Saturday evenings more and more people would gather in our shop, inevitably old Suslov, Barinov, Krotov the blacksmith and Migun. They would sit and have serious discussions. Then some would leave, to be replaced by others, and this went on almost until midnight.

Sometimes a drunk would start a brawl, most often this was an ex-soldier called Kostin, a one-eyed man with two fingers missing on his left hand. He would roll up his sleeves, wave his arms wildly and stride up to the shop like a fighting cock, hoarsely bellowing as hard as he could: 'Khokhol, they're a wicked nation, the Turks with their faith! Why don't you go to church, eh? You're a heretic and a trouble maker. Tell me, what kind of a man *are* you?'

Then they would all start teasing him.

'Mishka, why did you shoot your fingers off? Frightened of the Turks?'

He would square up for a fight, but the men would catch hold of him and laugh and shout as they pushed him into the gully. He would roll head over heels down the slope, screeching unbearably: 'Help, they've killed me! . . .'

Then, covered in dust, he would climb out and ask Khokhol for money for a glass of vodka.

'Why did you do that?' he asked.

'Just to amuse ourselves,' Kostin would answer. The peasants all laughed together.

One morning, during a holiday, when the cook had lit the firewood in the stove and had gone outside and while I was in the shop, I suddenly heard a very loud sigh from the kitchen. The whole shop shook, tins of caramels came clattering down from their shelves, broken window panes tinkled and there was a drumming noise on the floor. I rushed into the kitchen. Clouds of smoke came pouring out into the living room and through them I could hear something hissing and crackling. Khokhol seized me by the shoulder and said: 'Don't move.'

I could hear the cook howling outside in the hall.

'Oh, you stupid woman!' Khokhol shouted.

Romas dashed into the cloud of smoke and made a rattling sound with something. He swore loudly and shouted: 'Stop your howling. Get some water!'

Logs lay smoking on the floor, kindling wood burned and bricks were scattered here and there. The black mouth of the stove was empty, as though it had just been swept out. I groped around in the smoke for a bucket of water, poured it over the fire and started piling the logs back into the stove. 'Careful!' Khokhol said as he led the cook by the hand. He pushed her into the living room and ordered: 'Lock the shop. Be careful now, Maksimych, it might blow up again . . .'

And he squatted on the floor and began examining the

round fire logs. Then he started pulling out the logs I had just put into the stove.

'What are you doing?' I asked.

'Just look at this!'

He held out a strangely mutilated log and I could see that it had been hollowed out with a drill and that it had a particularly sooty look.

'Do you see? Those devils plugged them with gunpowder. Idiots! Now, what can you do with a pound of gunpowder?'

He put the log to one side and as he washed his hands he said: 'A good thing Aksinya went out, or she might have got hurt.'

The acrid smoke cleared away and I could see that the crockery on the shelves was smashed, all the window panes had been blown out and several bricks had been torn out of the mouth of the stove.

Khokhol's calmness at this time did not please me – he behaved as though that stupid trick did not worry him in the least. Village boys ran up and down the street and voices rang out: 'There's a fire at Khokhol's, we're burning!'

A woman moaned and wailed and Aksinya shouted anxiously from the kitchen: 'They're breaking into the shop, Mikhailo Antonych!'

'Be quiet,' he said, as he dried his wet beard on a towel. Hairy faces, distorted by fear and anger, peered through the open window, eyes screwed up from the biting smoke, and someone shouted in a shrill, excited voice: 'They should be driven out of the village! There's no just end to their mischief! What's going on?'

A small, red-haired peasant crossed himself and twitched his lips as he tried to climb through the window, but he did not succeed. He was holding an axe in his right hand and his left hand slipped every time he convulsively clutched at the window-sill.

Romas, who was holding a log, asked: 'Where do you think you're going?'

'To put the fire out!'

'But it's gone out'.

The peasant gaped in fright and disappeared. Romas went out to the steps at the front of the shop, held the log up and said to the crowd of people there: 'One of you stuffed this log with gunpowder and put it in with our firewood. But luckily there wasn't enough powder to do much damage.'

I stood behind Khokhol, looked at the crowd and heard the peasant with the axe say in a frightened voice: 'Just look at him waving that log at me.'

Kostin the soldier, who was already drunk, shouted: 'Get that lunatic out of here . . . arrest him . . .'

But most of the people said nothing as they stared at Romas and listened suspiciously to what he had to say: 'You need a *lot* of gunpowder to blow up a hut, yes, about thirty-six pounds! Come on now, clear off . . .'

Someone asked: 'Where's the head of the village?'

'Get a policeman!'

The people dispersed slowly, reluctantly, as though they were sorry about something.

We sat down to tea. Aksinya poured it out and I had never seen her looking so pleasant and kind: 'You never complain about them, so they start playing tricks.'

'Doesn't it make you angry?' I asked.

'There's no time to get angry over every stupid thing that happens.'

I thought to myself: If only everyone were as calm as her!

Khokhol had already announced that he was going to Kazan soon and he asked what books he could bring me back.

At times I though that instead of a soul this man had some sort of clockwork mechanism which had been wound up and set to run without stopping, all his life.

I loved Khokhol and deeply respected him, but I wanted him to get angry with me or someone else, to shout or stamp his feet, if only just once. However, either he was incapable of getting angry or he did not want to. When he was annoyed by some stupid behaviour or vile trick all he did was screw up his eyes sarcastically and say something that was invariably simple, and laconic, in brief, cold words.

For example, he once asked Suslov: 'Why do you always act against your conscience, old man?'

The old man's sallow cheeks and forehead slowly went purple and it seemed that even his white beard had turned red, right down to the roots.

'Well, it does *you* no good, and you'll lose people's respect.'

Suslov lowered his head and agreed: 'That's right, no good!'

Then he said to Izot: 'He's a spiritual leader. Men like him should be put in charge.'

In a few words Romas sensibly instructed me as to how I should behave while he was gone and it struck me that he had already forgotten the explosion they had tried to frighten him with, just as though it was nothing more terrible than being bitten by a fly.

Pankov arrived, inspected the stove and asked gloomily: 'Weren't you scared?'

'What of?'

'It's war!'

'Sit down and have some tea.'

'The wife's expecting me.'

'Where have you been?'

'Fishing. With Izot.'

He went into the kitchen and repeated, 'It's war', in the same pensive voice. He was very sparing in his words when he spoke to Khokhol, just as though he had long since talked over with him everything that was important and complicated. I remember Izot saying when I heard the history of the reign of Ivan the Terrible in Romas' version: 'A *boring* Tsar.'

'A butcher,' Kukushkin added, while Pankov announced in a determined voice: 'I can't see that there was anything particularly clever about *him*. Well, what if he did kill off princes and put a whole swarm of petty little noblemen in their place? What's more, he brought some into the country from abroad. Nothing clever about that. A small landowner is worse then a big one. A fly is no wolf, you can't kill it with a rifle, but it will cause you more trouble.'

Kukushkin appeared with a bucket of wet clay and said as he plastered the bricks back onto the stove: 'Look what they thought up, the devils! They can't get rid of their own lice, but when it comes to tormenting men ... You, Antonych, don't carry too much stock at once, better a little and more often, otherwise they'll burn the whole place down. You'll only have trouble, now you're getting that thing fixed up.'

'That thing' which the rich men in the village did not like was the market gardeners' cooperative. Khokhol had already nearly succeeded in setting it up with the help of Pankov, Suslov and two or three other sensible peasants. Most of the householders had grown more favourably inclined towards Romas and the number of customers in the shop had increased significantly. Even good-for-nothing peasants such as Barinov or Migun tried to help Khokhol's scheme in every way they could.

I liked Migun very much and loved his fine, sad songs. When he sang he would close his eyes, and his suffering face would stop twitching. He came alive on dark nights, when there was no moon or when the sky was covered with a thick pall of cloud. He used to call out to me softly when evening came: 'Come down to the Volga.'

There he would prepare his illegal tackle for sterlets, sitting at the stern of his little boat with his crooked, dark legs dangling in the water. He would whisper: 'When gentlemen make fun of me, all right, I can stand it, to hell with them. They know something I don't. But when my own brother, a peasant, cramps my style, how am I expected to take it? What's the difference between us? He counts his money in roubles, while I count it in kopecks, that's all.' Migun's face twitched in pain, his eyebrow jerked, his fingers moved quickly as he sharpened the fish hooks on a file and his soulful

voice range out softly: 'They think I'm a thief. That's true –
guilty! But doesn't everyone live by stealing? Doesn't everyone suck and nibble away at another? Yes, God doesn't love
us and the devil has fun!'

The dark river flowed past us and black clouds moved
above it. It was too dark to see the meadow banks, and the
waves beat cautiously against the sand and washed over my
feet, as though they were trying to carry me off into the limitless darkness that was swimming away somewhere . . .

'Is life necessary?' Migun asked with a sigh.

High up on a hill a dog barked mournfully. I asked myself,
as though in a dream, 'And why do you have to live the way
you do?'

It was very quiet on the river, completely dark and very
frightening. And there was no end to that warm darkness.

'They'll kill Khokhol. And you as well,' Migun muttered.
Then he suddenly started singing softly:

> 'My mother loved me . . .
> And used to say
> "Oh Yasha, my dearest one.
> Live a quiet life . . ."'

He would close his eyes, his voice became stronger and sadder, and his fingers moved more slowly as he sorted out the
twine in his tackle.

> 'I didn't listen to my mother,
> No, I didn't listen . . .'

I had a strange sensation, as though the earth had been washed
away by the heavy movement of that dark liquid mass and
was falling into it, while I myself was falling down, slipping
from the earth into the darkness where the sun had plunged
for ever.

Migun stopped singing just as suddenly as he had started
and he silently pulled the boat into the water, sat in it and
disappeared into the darkness with hardly a sound. I watched
him go and thought: Why do such people live?

Another friend of mine was Barinov, a lazy, slovenly man,

a braggart, slanderer and restless wanderer. He had lived in Moscow and would speak with disgust about it: 'A hellish city! Complete chaos. Churches – fourteen thousand and six of them, and all the people are swindlers. And they've got the mange like horses, I swear it! Merchants, householders – all of them go around scratching themselves. Yes, the Tsar cannon is there, an enormous gun. Peter the Great cast it himself to fire at rebels. One noblewoman stirred up a revolt against him – just out of love. He had lived with her for seven years, day in, day out, then he left her with three children. So she got angry and that's why she started a rebellion! Yes, my friend, he made a loud bang with the cannon and laid nine thousand three hundred and eight flat just with one shot! Even *he* was frightened. "No," he said to Metropolitan Philaret, "that devil's own thing must be sealed up, against temptation!" And so they sealed it . . .'

I told him that this was a lot of rubbish and this made him angry: 'Good God! What a nasty character you've got! A very learned man told me this story, in detail, yet you . . .'

He went on about how he had visited the saints in Kiev and told me: 'This city, like our village, stands on a hill, but I forget the name of the river. Just a puddle compared with the Volga! A complete mess of a town, to be honest. All the streets are crooked and all of them go uphill. The people are Ukrainians, not the same blood as Mikhailo Antonych, but half Polish, half Tartar. They don't talk, but gabble away. They don't comb their hair and they're dirty. They eat frogs that weigh ten pounds each there and ride their oxen and even use them for ploughing. These oxen are remarkable, even the smallest is still four times bigger than ours. They weigh three thousand pounds each. There's fifty-seven thousand monks there and two hundred and seventy-three bishops. Well, you're a strange one, how can you argue with this? I've seen it all with my own eyes. But were *you* ever there? No, you weren't. Well then! My dear friend, I love accuracy above all . . .'

He loved figures and I taught him how to add and multiply, but he could not stand division. He would enthusiastically mutiply compound figures and valiantly make one mistake after the other; then he would write out a long row of figures with his stick in the sand, look at them as though thunderstruck, goggling his child-like eyes, and exclaim: 'No one could even pronounce a thing like that!'

He was an ungainly man, dishevelled, with ragged clothes and his face, which was almost handsome, was framed by a curly, gay-looking beard. His eyes were light blue and shone with a child-like smile. He and Kukushkin had something in common and this must have been the reason for their avoiding each other.

Barinov had gone fishing twice in the Caspian Sea and he would start telling us deliriously: 'The sea, my friend, is different from anything else. You're only a midge compared with it! If you look at it, you are nothing! Life is sweet down by the sea, all kinds of people go there, even archimandrites: yes, I knew one who worked there like the rest of us! Then there was a cook who was the mistress of a public prosecutor – what more could anyone want? However, she pined for the sea and told him, "I like you very much, my prosecutor, but goodbye all the same!" That's because anyone who's seen the sea can't resist going back. There's such wide open spaces. It's like in the sky, no crowds. I'm going back – to stay. I don't like people, that's my trouble. I'd like to live like a hermit, in a hermitage somewhere. But I don't know any decent ones . . .'

He hung around the village like a stray dog, despised, but people listened to his stories with the same pleasure they derived from Migun's songs. 'He's an artful liar. Very entertaining!' they would say.

At times his fantasies disturbed the minds even of such down-to-earth people as Pankov. On one occasion that distrustful man told Khokhol: 'Barinov claims that books do not tell the whole truth about Ivan the Terrible. There's a lot that's covered up. It seems he could change his form, and he turned into an eagle, and that's why from that time onwards they stamped eagles on coins, in his honour.'

I noticed (and how many times!) that anything that was unusual, fantastic, often obviously clumsily concocted, pleased the people much more than serious stories about the real truth. But when I told Khokhol about this he grinned and said: 'But that will pass, the main thing is for people to learn how to think for themselves – then they might get near the truth. But you must try and understand eccentrics like Barinov and Kukushkin. They are artists, you know, authors. Christ must have been an eccentric, just like them. But you must agree that what *he* thought up wasn't so bad.'

I was amazed that all these people spoke so rarely and reluctantly about God. Only old Suslov would remark with firm conviction: 'Everything comes from God!' Always I sensed something hopeless in these words. I got on very well with these men and learned a lot from them during our nocturnal discussions. It seemed that each question Romas asked had planted its roots, like a mighty tree, into the very flesh of life and there, in its very heart, those roots would intertwine with roots from another equally ancient tree and on each branch thoughts would brightly blossom and the leaves of sonorous words richly unfurl themselves. I felt I was making great strides forward as I drank my fill of the stimulating honey of books, and I began to speak with more confidence. Khokhol grinned more than once and praised me: 'You're doing very well, Maksimych!'

How grateful I was to him for these words!

Sometimes Pankov would bring his wife along. She was a small woman with a gentle face and clever blue eyes. She used to dress in the 'town style' and sit quietly in one corner with her lips modestly pursed. But after a few moments her lips would open wide in surprise and her eyes dilate with fright. Sometimes, when she heard some pointed remark, she would laugh in embarrassment and cover her face with her hands.

Pankov would wink at Romas and say: 'She understands!' Cautious-looking people would come and visit Khokhol and he would take them up to my attic and sit there for hours.

Aksinya would take them food and drink and they would sleep there, unseen by anyone except the cook, who looked upon Romas with a dog-like devotion, almost idolizing him. At night-time Izot and Pankov would row these visitors in a small boat up to a passing steamboat or to the quay at Lobyshki. I would look down from the hill and watch the lentil-shaped boat flitting over the black river – now and again turned to silver by the moon – with its lamp swinging above to catch the steamboat captain's eye. I would look on, and feel that I was taking part in something great and mysterious.

Marya Derenkova would come down from the city but I no longer found anything embarrassing in the way she looked at me. Her eyes were like those of a girl happy in the consciousness of her own good looks and who was glad that a large, bearded man was courting her. He talked to her just as calmly and rather sarcastically as he did with everyone, only he stroked his beard more often and his eyes took on a warmer look.

Derenkova's thin little voice had a cheerful ring. She was dressed in a light blue frock with a pale blue ribbon in her hair. Her childish hands were strangely restless, as though searching for something to hold on to. She hummed some tune incessantly without opening her mouth as she fanned her rosy, languid face with a little handkerchief. There was something in her now that made me uneasy again, something hostile and angry. I tried to see as little of her as I could.

In the middle of July Izot disappeared. People said that he had drowned and two days later this was confirmed – about four miles downstream his boat – with its bottom smashed in and its side broken – was found washed up on the meadow bank. The explanation was thought to be that Izot had fallen asleep and his boat had collided with a group of three barges anchored three miles downstream from the village.

Romas was away in Kazan when this happened. In the evening Kukushkin came to the shop, gloomily sat down on some sacks, did not say one word, and then surveyed his feet, lit his pipe and asked: 'When's Khokhol coming back?'

'I don't know.'

He started rubbing his bruised face very hard with his palm and swore obscenely in a soft voice, snarling as though he were choking on a bone.

'What's the matter?' I asked.

He looked at me and bit his lips. His eyes turned red, his jaws trembled. When I saw that he was unable to speak I expected to hear something very sad and I felt deeply alarmed.

Finally he looked out into the street and after much difficulty managed to stammer: 'I was out with Migun. We looked at Izot's boat, the bottom was hacked through with an axe – understand? That means he was murdered! That's for sure!'

He shook his head and produced one obscenity after the other, punctuated by hollow-sounding but passionate sobs. Then he fell silent and started crossing himself. It was unbearable watching that man who wanted to cry but who was unable to. He was trembling all over and choking with anger and grief.

The next day some boys who were swimming in the river found Izot underneath a large wrecked barge lying grounded upstream from the village. Half of him was on the pebbles, the other in the water. Under the stern, caught on a piece of the smashed rudder, Izot's long body lay stretched out, face downwards, the skull crushed and empty: the water had washed the brains from it. Someone had struck Izot from behind on the back of his skull and one could see where it had been split open by an axe. The current swayed his body, moving his legs and arms towards the bank, so it seemed that he was making a strong effort to clamber out onto the shore. About twenty miserable faced, wealthy peasants gathered in a group on the river bank – the poor peasants had not yet returned from the fields. The village elder, a cowardly thieving man, stood there waving his staff, sniffing and wiping his nose on his pink shirt-sleeve.

Kuzmin, a thick-set shopkeeper, stood there with his legs wide apart and his belly sticking out. He looked at me and Kukushkin in turn and frowned threateningly, but his colourless eyes were full of tears and his pock-marked face was pathetic. 'What a lousy thing to happen!' the village elder moaned and danced up and down with his crooked legs.

'Oh, it's very bad.' His plump daughter-in-law sat on a stone, peered blankly into the water, and crossed herself with trembling fingers. Her lips twitched and the lower lip, which was thick and red, and hung just like a dog's, revealed her yellow, sheep-like teeth.

Girls and young boys came rushing down the hillside, making bright splashes of colour and dust-covered peasants hurried in from the field. The crowd made a soft buzzing sound.

'He was always picking a quarrel.'

'Who?'

'That Kukushkin – he's a trouble-maker.'

'They killed a man for no reason at all.'

'Izot never harmed anyone!'

'Never harmed anyone?' Kukushkin yelled and turned on the crowd.

'Then why did you have to kill him, eh, you scum! Eh?'

Some peasant woman broke into hysterical laughter and this seemed to lash the crowd like a whip. The peasants turned on each other, bawling, roaring and cursing. Kukushkin leaped up to the shopkeeper, swung his arm and hit him on his rough cheek with the palm of his hand.

'Take that, you animal!'

By swinging his fists he soon battled his way through the brawling crowd. Then he shouted to me almost cheerfully: 'Get out of here, there's going to be a fight!'

Someone had already hit him and he spat blood from his broken lip. However, his face glowed with satisfaction. 'Did you see how I bashed Kuzmin?' Barinov came running up, took a frightened look at the crowd which was packed close together near the barge, and above all the noise I could hear the elder's thin voice: 'No, you prove it, if I've shown favour to anyone. Prove it.'

'I must get out of here,' Barinov growled as we climbed up the slope. It was a very hot evening and the air was so heavy it was hard to breathe. The crimson-coloured sun was setting among dense, bluish clouds and gleaming red patches of light were reflected on the leaves of the bushes. Somewhere I could hear thunder rumbling.

Right in front of me Izot's body moved to and fro; the hair on his smashed skull had been straightened by the current, and seemed to be standing on end.

I remember his low voice and the fine words he used: 'There's something childish in every man, *that*'s what you must see as the important thing. Take Khokhol: you'd think he was made of iron, but he has the soul of a child!'

As he strode along beside me Kukushkin said angrily: 'They'll do the same to all of us. God, what stupidity!'

About two days later Khokhol turned up late in the night and he was clearly very pleased about something and unusually friendly.

When I had let him into the hut he slapped me on the shoulder and said: 'You don't get enough sleep, Maksimych!'

'Izot's been murdered.'

'Wha-at?'

Knots of muscle swelled out on his cheeks and his beard quivered and seemed to cascade onto his chest. Without taking his cap off he stopped in the middle of the room, blinking and shaking his head: 'So, they don't know who it was then? Yes, of course.'

He slowly went over to the window and sat there with his legs planted wide apart.

'Well, I kept warning him . . . have the authorities been?'

'The local constable came yesterday.'

Then he asked: 'Well, what happened?' and he answered his own question: 'Of course – nothing!'

I told him that, as always, the policeman had stopped at Kuzmin's and ordered him to be put in the 'cooler' for hitting the shopkeeper.

'So. And what can you say to that?'

I went into the kitchen to heat the samovar.

While we were having tea Romas said: 'I feel sorry, this nation – they kill their own best people! You'd think they were afraid of them – "not needed", as they say around here. When I trod the stage to Siberia one convict told me that he was a thief and had a gang working for him, there were five of them. One of the gang said: "Let's stop robbing people. There's no sense in it, we still have a rotten life!" For saying this they strangled him while he was in a drunken sleep. The man who told this story spoke very highly of the murdered man. "I polished off another three after that," he told me, "and it doesn't bother me. But I feel sorry for my friend to this day. A good man, clever, cheerful, with a fine soul." And I asked, "Why did you kill him then? Frightened he would give you away?" Do you know, he took offence at this and said, "No, he wouldn't have betrayed us for any price, not for anything! But we felt uncomfortable with someone like that around. We were all sinners and he seemed to be the righteous one. It didn't seem right."'

Khokhol got up and started striding round the room with his hands behind his back. He held a pipe between his teeth and was dressed in a long white, Tartar smock which reached right down to his ankles. He stepped firmly with his bare feet and said in a soft thoughtful voice: 'I've met this fear of honest men time and again, this destruction of a good man. You can deal with people like this in two ways: either you try to finish them off one way or the other after worrying the life out of them first, or, like dogs, you look them straight in the face and crawl in front of them on your belly. But that's not

137

so common. And if people try to live with them, to imitate them, they can't and they don't know how to. Perhaps they don't want to!' He picked up a glass of tea that had gone cold and added: 'Yes, perhaps they don't want to! Just think, it cost people a lot of trouble to make some sort of life for themselves and they got used to it. Then along comes someone who rebels and says they shouldn't live like that. "Not like this?" they say. "But we have put all the strength we have into it, to hell with you!" So they get rid of the teacher, the righteous man. "Don't interfere," they say. But the fact remains, those who say "don't live like this" are right. And they are the ones who improve life.'

He waved his arm at a row of books and added: 'Especially these! Oh, if only I could write a book, but I'm no good at that kind of thing. My thoughts are clumsy, all mixed up.'

He sat down at the table, propped himself on his elbows, pressed his hands on his head and said: 'I'm so sorry about Izot . . .'

After a long silence he said: 'Come on, let's get some sleep.'

I went back to my attic and sat by the window. Summer lightning flashed over the fields and flooded half of the sky. It seemed that the moon shook with fear when that transparent, reddish light poured over the sky. Dogs barked and howled in a heart-rending way. If it had not been for that howling I could easily have imagined myself on a desert island. Distant thunder rumbled and a heavy current of stifling heat poured through the window. Izot's body lay before me under an osier bush on the bank. His blue face was turned towards the sky and his glassy eyes seemed to be looking sternly inwards. His golden beard was matted into pointed tufts and his mouth, wide open in astonishment, was hiding in it.

'The chief thing, Maksimych, is kindness, affection! I love Easter because it is the most friendly holiday!'

Izot's blue trousers which had dried out in the scorching sun clung to his legs, washed clean by the Volga. Flies buzzed over the fisherman's face and a strong, nauseating smell came from his body. I could hear heavy footsteps on the stairs and Romas came in, bending low under the doorway. He sat on my bunk and gathered his beard into his hand.

'Well, did you know I'm getting married? Oh, yes.'

'It's going to be hard for a woman here,' I replied.

He stared at me as though he had expected me to say something else. The reflections from the lightning flashed into the room and filled it with a transparent light.

'I'm going to marry Masha Derenkova.'

I could not help smiling. Up to that minute the thought had never occurred to me that one could call that girl Masha. I do not remember her father or her brothers ever calling her Masha.

'What are you laughing at?'

'Nothing.'

'Do you think I'm too old for her?'

'Oh, no!'

'She told me *you* were in love with her.'

'Yes, it seems I was.'

'And now? Has it passed?'

'Yes, I think so.'

He let go his beard and said softly, 'That often happens at your age, not at mine. It just takes a complete hold on you so you can't think about anything else – there's no strength left!'

He bared his fine teeth into a smile and went on: 'Antony lost the battle of Actium to Octavius because he abandoned his fleet and command, and he sailed after Cleopatra in his warship when she got frightened and fled from the battle – that's the kind of thing that can happen!'

Romas stood up, straightened himself and repeated, as though acting against his will: 'So, whatever happens, I'm getting married!'

'Soon?'

'In the autumn, when the apples are finished.'

He went away, lowering his head under the door more

139

than he needed to, while I got into bed and thought it would be best if I left in the autumn. But why did he say all that about Antony? I did not like that.

The time for picking the fast-ripening apples was not far off. There was a rich harvest and the branches of the trees bowed down to the ground under the weight of the fruit. An acrid smell enveloped the orchard, children made a loud noise as they gathered the maggoty and wind-fallen yellow and pink apples. Early in August Romas returned from Kazan in a flat-bottomed boat laden with merchandise and with another full of boxes. It was eight o'clock on a weekday morning. Khokhol had just changed and washed. As he began his tea he said cheerfully: 'It's lovely sailing down the river at night.'

Suddenly he stuck his nose out and asked anxiously: 'Do you think you can smell burning?'

At that moment I heard Aksinya wailing in the yard: 'We're on fire!' We rushed outside. One wall of the shed was burning from the side nearest the kitchen window – in this shed we stored kerosene, tar and oil. For a few moments we looked thunderstruck as the yellow tongues of fire, pale in the bright sunlight, licked the wall in a business-like way and curled up towards the roof. Aksinya brought a bucket of water, Khokhol emptied it over the fiery blossoms on the wall, dropped it and said: 'That's no good! Roll the barrels out, Maksimych! Aksinya – into the shop!'

I quickly rolled a barrel of tar out into the yard and into the street and got hold of a barrel of kerosene. But when I turned it over I found that the bung was missing and the kerosene poured out onto the ground. The fire did not linger and sharp wedges of flames licked through the wooden planks of the shed. The roof began to crackle and something seemed to be singing and mocking me. I rolled out the half-empty barrel and saw that from every part of the village women and children were running all along the street, howling and screaming. Khokhol and Aksinya dragged goods out of the shop and piled them up in the gully. A grey-haired old woman dressed in black stood in the middle of the street waving her fist menacingly and shrieked: 'Oh, you devils!'

When I got back to the shed I found it filled with dense smoke from the middle of which came a humming, cracking sound; red ribbons twisted and curled down from the roof. The wall had already become nothing more than an incandescent lattice. The smoke blinded and choked me, and I hardly had the strength to roll the barrel up to the door of the shed. There it got stuck and I was unable to budge it. Sparks showered down from the roof and burned my skin. I called out for help. Khokhol came running, seized me by the hand and pushed me out into the yard.

'Get out before it explodes!'

He threw himself into the hall, I rushed after him, and dashed up to my attic where I kept a lot of my books. After I had thrown them out of the window I wanted to hurl a hatbox after them, but the window was too narrow. So I started knocking the frame out with a heavy weight. But then there was a dull bang, something splashed violently against the roof and I realized that the kerosene barrel had exploded. The roof above my head was blazing away and cracking, and a reddish stream of fire poured past my window and peered into it on its way. The heat became intolerable. I ran to the stairs, but I was met by thick clouds of smoke. Crimson snakes slithered over the steps, while down below in the entrance hall there was a crunching sound, as though iron teeth were eating into a tree. I panicked and just stood there without moving for several minutes, blinded by the smoke, hardly able to breathe. A yellow face with a red beard peered through the dormer window above the stairs. It twisted convulsively and immediately disappeared. The next moment blood-coloured spears of flame broke through the roof. It seemed, as I now remember, that the hair on my head was crackling and I could hear nothing else. I realized that I was lost, my legs grew heavy and my eyes smarted badly, although I covered them with my hands.

But life's wise instinct for survival showed me the only way to escape. I seized my mattress and pillow and a bunch of bast in my arms, wrapped Romas' sheepskin coat over my head and jumped out of the window.

I regained consciousness at the edge of the gully and found Romas squatting in front of me and crying: 'Wha-at?'

I stood up and felt that I was going mad as I watched the hut growing smaller, with red splinters falling all round it. Crimson dog tongues of fire were licking the black earth in front of it. Black smoke poured out of the windows and yellow flowers rocked to and fro as they blossomed on the roof. 'Well, are you all right?' Khokhol shouted. His face, covered in sweat and smeared with soot, was weeping dirty tears and his eyes blinked in fright. Pieces of bast were tangled up with his beard. A refreshing wave of joy swept over me – such a tremendous sensation! – and then I felt a searing pain in my left foot. I lay down and told Khokhol: 'I've dislocated my foot.' He felt it and suddenly gave it a sharp jerk. A terrible pain shot through me and a few minutes later, drunken with joy (although limping slightly) I was carrying the things that had been saved along to the bath-house, while Romas said cheerfully, his pipe clenched between his teeth: 'I was sure you would be burned to death when that barrel blew up and the kerosene splashed on the roof. The flames shot up in a column, very big they were and then an enormous mushroom appeared in the sky and the whole hut was swallowed up by the fire. Well, I thought that was the last of Maksimych!' By now he had calmed down again, as always, methodically piling some things into a heap and telling the grubby, dishevelled Aksinya: 'Sit here and watch this lot while I go and pour more water . . .' White pieces of paper fluttered about in the smoke over the gully.

'Oh!' Romas said, 'I'm sorry about the books. They were my very own . . .' Four huts were already burning. There was not much wind so the fire took its time; it spread left and right and sent out supple little creepers that seemed to hook onto fences and roofs with reluctance. A fiery comb scraped at the thatched roof. Crooked, fiery fingers ran over the wattle fences and played on them as though they were psalteries. In that smoky air I could hear the evil, whinnying, passionate song of the flames and the soft, almost tender crackling of smouldering timber. Golden embers fell out from the clouds of smoke onto the street and yards, and peasant men and women rushed around in wild confusion, concerned only for their own property and setting up a non-stop wailing: 'Water!'

But water was far away, down the hill, in the Volga. Romas quickly herded some peasants together, seizing them by the shoulder and shoving them along. Then he divided them into two groups and ordered them to break down the fences and outbuildings along both sides of the fire. They obeyed him submissively and now they tackled the fire more sensibly as it confidently tried to devour the whole street. But all the same, they went about the job apprehensively, without any hope, as though doing someone else's work.

Now I was in a joyful mood and I felt stronger than ever before. At the end of the street I noticed a crowd of rich peasants with the village elder Kuzmin at their head. They just stood there idly like spectators, shouting and waving arms and sticks. Peasants rode in from the fields waving their elbows high as their ears. Howling women went to meet them and the village boys started scampering all over the place. The outbuildings in another yard caught fire and it was necessary to chop down the walls of a shed as soon as possible. This was made of thick wattle and it was already decorated with crimson ribbons of fire. The peasants started hacking down the fence, but sparks and burning embers came showering down on them and they sprang back, rubbing their shirts with the palms of their hands.

'Don't be cowards!' shouted Khokhol.

But this did not help. So he tore someone's cap off and pressed it down over my head.

'Start chopping from this end, I'll start from here!'

I hacked through two stakes, one after the other, and the wall began to shake. I then scrambled up it and tried to catch hold of the top, but Khokhol pulled me back by my legs and the whole wall fell in, covering me almost up to my head. The peasants threw the wattle out into the street.

'Get burnt?' Romas asked.

His anxiety only increased my agility and strength. I wanted to excel in front of this man who was so dear to me and I worked furiously, just to earn his praise. Above us pages from our books were still flying around in the smoke like pigeons. On the right we succeeded in checking the fire, but on the left it spread even further, engulfing a tenth yard. Romas left some of the peasants to follow the crafty meanderings of the red snakes and then he drove most of the men to the area on the left. As we ran past the rich peasants I heard someone shout maliciously: 'It's arson!' while the shopkeeper said: 'Better look in his bath-house!' These words settled unpleasantly in my memory.

Everyone knows that excitement – especially joyful excitement – increases one's strength. I *was* excited and I worked oblivious of everything and finally exhausted myself. I remember sitting on the ground and leaning against something hot. Romas poured water out of a bucket over me, while the peasants formed a circle round us and respectfully muttered: 'He's a strong boy!'

'He won't let you down.'

I pressed my head to Romas' leg and burst into shameful tears. He stroked my head and said: 'Have a rest. You've done enough.'

Kukushkin and Barinov, black as devils with soot, led me away into the gully and tried to console me:

'It's nothing, it's all over now.'

'Frightened?'

I had hardly time to lie down and come to my senses when I saw ten of the 'rich ones' going down into the gully, towards our bath-house. At their head was the village elder, while behind him two local policemen were leading Romas by the arm. He had no cap, one sleeve of his wet shirt had been torn off, his pipe was still sticking between his teeth, and his face frowned grimly. He looked terrifying. Kostin the soldier shook a stick and roared furiously: 'Into the fire with him, the heretic!'

'Open up the bath-house.'

'Smash the lock, the key's lost,' Romas said in a loud voice.

I leaped up, seized a wooden stake that was lying on the ground and stood at his side. The policemen moved away, while the village elder cried in a shrill, frightened voice: 'God-fearing people, you are not allowed to break locks!'

Kuzmin pointed at me and shouted: 'Here's another one now . . . who is he?'

'Take it easy, Maksimych,' Romas said. 'They think I hid goods in the bath-house and set fire to the shop.'

'It was the two of you!'

'Break the lock!'

'God-fearing people . . .'

'We'll answer!'

'Our answer is . . .'

Romas whispered: 'Stand with your back to mine so they can't hit you from behind.'

They broke the bath-house lock and a few men squeezed through the door, but almost immediately they came out again. Meanwhile I shoved my stake into Romas' hand and picked another up.

'Nothing there.'

'Nothing?'

'Ah, the crafty devils!'

Someone said timidly: 'It's no good.'

And he was answered by some wild, apparently drunken voices: 'Why is it no good?'

'Into the fire with them!'

'Trouble makers.'

'Making their own guilds!'

'Thieves! The whole lot of them are thieves.'

'Stop it!' roared Romas. 'You've seen with your own eyes that I've nothing hidden in the bath-house – what more proof do you want? Everything's burnt, you can see what's been saved, can't you? And why should I set fire to my own property?'

'It's for the insurance!'

And once again a dozen voices yelled violently: 'No point in just looking at them!'

'Enough! Our patience is gone! ...'

My legs shook and everything went dark for a moment. I could see wild faces through that reddish mist, with hairy holes for mouths, and I had difficulty in stopping myself from hitting those people. They kept on shouting and jumping around us.

'Oh ho, they've got stakes!'

'Stakes!?'

'They'll tear my beard off,' Khokhol said, and I sensed that he was smiling. 'And you'll cop it too, Maksimych! But take it easy, easy ...'

'Look, the young one's got an axe!'

In actual fact I had an axe hanging from my belt, which I had forgotten about. 'They look frightened now,' Romas said. 'But don't use that axe if they start something ...'

An unfamiliar, small, insignificant-looking peasant with a limp danced about comically and squealed furiously: 'Chuck bricks at them from here! Come on, hit me on the head!'

He put his words into action, picked up a piece of brick and caught me in the stomach. But before I could reply Kukushkin flew down onto him like a hawk and they rolled down the gully locked together. Pankov, Barinov, the smith and about another ten men ran after Kukushkin. Immediately I heard Kukushkin say in a dignified voice: 'You, Mikhaylo Antonov, are a clever man and you should know that fires make men go mad . . .' Romas said: 'Maksimych, let's go down to the pub on the river bank.' He took his pipe out of his mouth and with a sharp jerk shoved it into a trouser pocket. Using the stake to lean on he wearily climbed out of the gully and when Kuzmin (who was walking at his side) said something, he answered without looking at him: 'Clear off, you fool!'

On the place where our hut had been a golden heap of embers was smouldering. In the middle the stove was still standing. The pipe had survived as well and light blue wisps of smoke drifted out of it into the hot air. The red hot bars of a bunk stuck out like spider's legs. Charred door posts stood by the fire like black watchmen, and one of them seemed to be wearing a red hat of embers and small flames, like a cock's feathers.

'My books are all burnt,' Khokhol said with a sigh. 'That's annoying!' The village boys pushed large charred logs out into the muddy street, just as though they were piglets and they hissed and fizzled out, filling the air with an acrid, whitish smoke. One of the boys, about five years old and with light blue eyes and fair hair, sat in a warm black puddle beating a dented bucket with a stick and listening to the sound of the blows on the metal with intense enjoyment. The peasants, who had lost everything in the fire, walked around gloomily and piled up what was left of their domestic possessions into little heaps. Women cried and swore, and quarrelled over a few charred bits of wood. The trees in the gardens behind the scene of the fire stood motionless and on many of them the foliage had turned reddish-brown from the heat – one could see the rich crop of rosy apples more easily now.

We went down to the river, had a swim and then we sat silently drinking tea in the pub on the bank.

Romas said: 'Those blood-suckers have lost their apples now . . .'

Pankov came up, looking more pensive and subdued than ever.

'Well, my friend?' Khokhol asked.

Pankov shrugged his shoulders and said: 'My hut was insured.'

No one said anything, and we peered at each other inquiringly, just like strangers.

'What will you do now, Mikhail Antonych?'

'I'll have to think about it.'

'You should get out of here.'

'I'll see.'

Pankov said: 'I have a plan, let's go outside and talk it over on our own.'

They went off. Pankov paused at the door and told me: 'Can't say you're shy! You'll be all right here – they'll be frightened of you . . .'

I went down to the river bank as well, lay down under some bushes and looked at the river. It was still hot, although the sun was already setting in the west. My whole life in the village unfolded before me in a broad scroll, and seemed to be painted on the surface of the river. I felt sad. But tiredness soon got the upper hand and I fell fast asleep.

'Hey,' I heard someone shouting through my sleep and I felt that someone was shaking and dragging me off somewhere. 'Are you dead? Wake up!'

A purple moon shone over the meadows, large as a wheel. Barinov was leaning over me and shaking me.

'Come on now, Khokhol's looking for you. He's worried!'

He grumbled as he walked behind me.

'You've no right to fall asleep just where you like. Supposing someone comes up the hill and stumbles – a stone might fall on you. Or they might do it on purpose. We're not the joking sort. People have a good memory for wrong done to them. Besides that, they've got nothing to remember anyway.'

Someone was quietly moving around in the bushes on the river bank and I saw the branches shake.

'Found him?' I heard Migun's rich voice asking.

'I'll take you to him,' Barinov answered.

He walked a few paces away and then said with a sigh: 'He's going poaching for fish. Migun's life isn't easy either.'

Romas rebuked me angrily when he came up: 'What are you roaming around for? Looking for a good hiding?'

When we were alone Romas said in a soft, gloomy voice: 'Pankov is offering you a place with him. He wants to open a shop. But I don't advise you to go. Listen, I sold him everything that was left. I'm going to Vyatka and in a short while I'll write for you to come. All right?'

'I'll think about it,' I replied.

'Think then.'

He lay on the floor, fidgeted a little and then was silent. I sat at the window looking at the Volga. The moon's reflection reminded me of the flames in the fire. Over by the meadows a steam tug heavily splashed its paddles. Three mast lamps sailed along in the darkness and seemed to touch the stars, blotting them out at times.

'Are you annoyed with the peasants?' Romas asked sleepily. 'You shouldn't be. They're stupid, that's all. Now malice is a stupid thing.'

His words did not bring me any comfort and did nothing to soften my fury and sharp sense of injury. Again I saw before me animal-like mouths with hair growing round them, belching out their vicious cries: 'Throw some bricks from where we're standing.'

At this time I still could not forget things best forgotten. I saw very well that, in each of those people, taken individually, there was not very much malice, often none at all. They were essentially good-hearted animals and it was not difficult to make any one of them smile like a child, and any one of them would listen to stories about quests for intellect and happiness, about the great exploits of magnanimous men with the credulity of children. Everything that aroused dreams of an easy life, in which man's will was the only law, was dear to their strange souls.

But when they gathered in one grey mass at village assemblies or in the pub on the river bank, they left behind all that was fine in them and they dressed themselves like priests in vestments of lies and hypocrisy. Some dog-like desire to please the strong ones in the village took possession of them and then it disgusted me to look at them. They would suddenly be seized by fits of wolfish spite and would bristle up, with teeth bared. Then they would howl wildly at each other, ready for a fight – and they would fight, over any trifle. At these moments they were terrifying and they seemed capable of destroying the very church where only the previous evening they had gathered humbly and submissively, like sheep in a fold.

They had their own poets and storytellers, who were loved by no one, and who were the laughing-stock of the whole village, helpless and despised.

I just could not go on living with such people and I poured out all my bitter thoughts to Romas on the same day we parted.

'A hasty conclusion,' he said reproachfully.

'But what can I do, if I'm firmly convinced of it?'

'An erroneous conclusion. Unfounded.'

For a long time he kept trying to convince me with his fine words that I was wrong, that I had made a mistake.

'Don't judge hastily. Judging others is the easiest thing in the world, so don't get carried away by it. Look at everything calmly and remember one thing: everything passes, everything changes for the better. You say *slowly*? Yes, and for that reason it *lasts*! Poke your nose in everywhere, feel everything out for yourself. Fear nothing, but don't judge hastily. Goodbye, my dear little friend!'

We met again fifteen years later in Sedlets, after Romas had served a ten-year sentence in Yakutsk for being mixed up with the 'People's Right' party. A heavy, leaden feeling of weariness took hold of me when he left Krasnovidovo and I wandered around the village just like a young puppy that had lost its master.

I went round the countryside with Barinov, working for rich peasants, threshing, digging potatoes, clearing gardens.

I lived in his bath-house. 'Aleksei Maksimych – a leader without any followers. Right?' he asked me one rainy evening. 'Shall we go down to the sea tomorrow? Good heavens, nothing to stay here for! They don't like our kind, you never know what they might get up to when they're drunk.'

This was not the first time Barinov had said this. He too was miserable. His ape-like hands drooped impotently, and he kept on looking round gloomily, as though he had lost his way in a forest. Rain lashed against the bath-house window and a stream of water washed away at one corner and flowed in a noisy torrent down to the bottom of the gully. The pale lightning of the last storm flickered feebly. Barinov asked softly: 'Shall we go then? Tomorrow?'

And so we went.

I cannot describe how wonderful it was to sail down the Volga on an autumn night, sitting at the stern of a barge steered by a hairy monster with an enormous beard, tapping his heavy feet on the deck and sighing deeply:

'Oh-oop! O-rro . . . oo . . .'

The water gently lapped behind the stern in a silky stream, thick as resin, and appeared to be boundless. Black autumnal clouds swirled over the river. Nothing else seemed to exist besides the slow motion of the darkness which blotted out the river banks. It seemed that the whole earth had melted away into it and was transformed into something smoky and liquid, flowing downwards in an unending, unbroken stream with all its heavy mass into a silent expanse where there was no sun, nor moon, nor stars . . .

Ahead, in the damp darkness, the invisible steam tug panted as it painfully toiled away, as though trying to resist the resilient force that was drawing it on. Three lights – two over the water and one high up above the others – led it on its way. Another four swam nearer to me, under the rain clouds, just like golden carp, and one of them was the lamp on the mast of our barge. I felt as though I was enclosed in a cold, oily bubble which was gently sliding downhill and I was caught in it, like a midge. It seemed that the ship was slowing down, and the moment was near when it would come to a complete halt. Then the tug would stop grumbling and beating its paddles through the heavy waters and all sounds would fall away like leaves from a tree and would be obliterated like chalk inscriptions. Then immobility and silence would hold me in their majestic embrace. And that large man in his torn sheepskin jacket and a tattered hat, pacing about at the rudder, would stop quite still, under a perpetual spell, and he would never cry again: 'Orr-up! Ooo-urr!'

I asked him: 'What's your name?'

'What's that to you?' he replied in a dull voice.

As we sailed away from Kazan I noticed in the sunset that this man was as clumsy as a bear, had a hairy face without any eyes. As he stood over the rudder he would empty a bottle of vodka into a wooden jug and polish it off in just two swigs like water and then bite into an apple. When the tug jerked the barge this man would clutch the rudder, peer at the red disc of the sun, shake his head and say: 'God be blessed!'

The tug was towing four barges from the fair at Nizhny to Astrakhan. They were laden with iron, barrels of sugar and some very heavy boxes – all destined for Persia. Barinov tapped the boxes with his foot, sniffed and said: 'Must be rifles from the Izhev factory.'

But the man at the rudder prodded him in the stomach with his fist and asked: 'What's that to do with you?'

'It was just in my thoughts . . .'

'Would you like it in the face as well?'

We did not have the money to pay the fares by passenger boat and we had been taken on board 'out of kindness' and although we 'kept watch' with the sailors, everyone on that barge looked on us as beggars.

Barinov said reproachfully: 'And you talk about the people. It's quite simple, the one in the driving seat comes out on top . . .'

The darkness was so intense that the other barges were invisible, except for the tips of the masts lit up by their lanterns against the background of clouds of smoke that smelled of oil.

I was irritated by the helmsman's gloomy silence. But the boatswain had given me the job of keeping watch with that animal at the rudder. As he watched the lights swinging round the river bends he softly said: 'Hey, take hold!'

I would leap to my feet and turn the rudder.

'That's fine,' he would growl.

And I would sit down on the deck again. It was impossible to hold a conversation with that man, since all he did was ask: 'What's that to do with you?'

What *was* he thinking about? When we passed a place where the yellow waters of the Kama merged with the steely ribbon of the Volga he looked towards the north and growled: 'Scum . . .'

'Who?'

He did not answer.

Somewhere far off, in the depths of the darkness, dogs howled and barked, a reminder that there were still traces of life not yet completely stifled by the dark. They seemed quite beyond reach and unwanted here.

'The dogs here are nasty,' the man at the rudder suddenly said:

'Where . . . here?'

'Everywhere. Where I came from they have *real* dogs.'

'Where's that?'

'Vologda.'

And the grey, heavy words poured out, just like potatoes from a broken sack. 'Who's that with you – your uncle? In my opinion he's a fool. But my uncle's clever, and dashing, and rich. Owns a jetty at Simbirsk, and a pub. On the river bank.' He said all this very slowly, and apparently with difficulty, then stared with invisible eyes at the lamp on the mast and watched it crawling in the web of darkness like a golden spider.

'Catch hold . . . well, can you read and write? Don't you know who writes the laws?'

Without waiting for an answer he went on: 'Some say it's the Tsar, some say the Metropolitan, some the Senate. If I knew for sure I would go and see him and say: "You write the laws in such a way that I can't even take a swing, let alone hit someone! Laws must be like iron. Like a lock. They've locked my heart up and that's the end of it!" This would be my answer. But in this way I can't even answer. Oh no!'

He mumbled to himself, ever more softly and incoherently as he tapped his fist on the wooden lever.

Someone hailed on a loudspeaker from the tug and the dull voice of a man seemed just as out of place as the dogs' howling and barking which had already been sucked in by the richness of the night.

Oily, yellow reflections of the lamps drifted and melted away by the sides of the tug, incapable of casting light on anything. And those dense, viscous dark clouds, heavy with rain, floated over our heads like sediment.

Deeper and deeper we slipped into the silent depths of darkness. The helmsman gloomily complained: 'What have they brought me to? My heart can't breathe . . .'

I was overcome by indifference – indifference and dreary yearning. I just wanted to sleep.

A weak, grey sunless dawn struggled through the clouds, and wearily crept up the sky. It turned the water a leaden colour and showed up yellow bushes on the river banks, iron-like pines with trunks covered with rust, their branches like black paws, a row of village huts, the figure of a peasant who seemed to be carved out of stone. The crooked feathers of a seagull whistled as it flew over the barge.

The helmsman and myself were relieved from our watch and I crawled under a tarpaulin and fell asleep. But very soon (or so it seemed) I was awakened by the sound of stamping and shouting. I poked my head out and saw three sailors pressing the helmsman against the wall of a cabin and shouting in a mixed chorus: 'Drop it, Petrukha!'

'Good God – don't *worry*!'

'That's enough from you!'

The helmsman stood there quite calmly with arms crossed and his fingers digging into his shoulders. He pressed some bundle down onto the deck with one foot, looked at everyone in turn and implored them hoarsely: 'Let me escape from sin!'

He was barefooted, without any hat, just shirt and trousers. A dark mass of uncombed hair stuck out and fell down over his stubborn protruding forehead. Underneath that mess one could see his tiny, mole-like eyes, which were bloodshot and had an imploring, uneasy look.

'You'll drown,' they were saying to him.

'Me? Never. Let me go, brothers. If you don't I'll kill him! As soon as we get to Simbirsk ... I'll ...'

'Now stop it!'

'Oh, brothers ...'

He slowly spread his arms wide apart, fell down on his knees, touched the cabin wall with his arms as though he were being crucified and repeated: 'Let me escape from sin!'

There was something really staggering in his peculiarly deep voice. His parted arms were as long as oars and his hands trembled with outstretched palms. His bear-like face quivered in its frame of shaggy beard and his mole-like blind eyes bulged out of their sockets like tiny dark balls. It seemed that some unseen hand had gripped him by the throat and was choking him.

The peasants silently made way for him. He clumsily got to his feet, lifted the bundle and said: 'Well, thank you.'

He went to the side and jumped into the river with unexpected ease. I rushed to the side as well and saw Petrukha's head moving. He had placed the bundle on it like a hat and was swimming diagonally across the river towards a sandy bank where bushes, bowing under the wind, leaned forward to meet him and cast their yellow leaves into the water. The peasants said: 'So he got a grip of himself after all!'

'Has he gone mad?' I asked.

'Gone mad? No, he's done that to save his soul . . .'

Petrukha had already reached a shallow spot, stood breast deep in the water and waved his bundle over his head.

The sailors shouted: 'Good – by – ye!'

Someone asked: 'What will he do without a passport?'

A red-haired bandy-legged sailor took great pleasure in telling me: 'In Simbirsk he has a rotten uncle who cheated him out of everything. So he made up his mind to kill him. Yes. But in the end he saved himself and escaped from sin. Peasants are like wild animals, but they are good-hearted. He's a good man . . .'

And now that good man was already striding upstream along a narrow strip of sand, and then he disappeared into the bushes.

The sailors turned out to be very kind – they were all from the same district as myself and they had lived along the Volga from time immemorial. By the evening I was feeling quite at home among them. But the next day I noticed that they were looking at me gloomily, distrustfully. I guessed immediately that the devil had pulled Barinov's tongue and that this dreamer had told the bargees something.

'Have you been saying anything to them?' I asked.

With a smile in his womanish eyes he scratched himself behind one ear in embarrassment and confessed: 'I told them a *little*!'

'And didn't I tell you to keep quiet?'

'I did, but it was such an interesting story. We wanted to play cards but the helmsman took them and it became terribly boring! So I told them . . .'

From my cross-examination it became clear that Barinov, from sheer boredom, had concocted a very amusing story, at the end of which Khokhol and myself appeared fighting a crowd of peasants with axes, like ancient Vikings.

It was impossible to feel angry with him – truth for him was beyond reality. Once, when I was out with him looking for work and had sat down to rest on the edge of a gully, in a persuasive, friendly voice, he started exhorting me: 'You have to find your own kind of truth, for yourself. Look over there beyond the gully – a herd's grazing, a dog's running around, a shepherd's walking. Well, what of it? What food for our souls is there? My dear boy, just look: evil men are the truth, but where are the good ones? Not even invented yet, oh no!'

At Simbirsk the sailors, in the most unfriendly way, told us to get off the boat.

'We don't want your kind,' they said.

They rowed us to the jetties at Simbirsk and we dried ourselves out on the bank. We had thirty-seven kopecks in our pockets.

Then we went off to a pub for some tea.

'What shall we do now?' I asked.

Barinov said convincingly: 'Well, what then? We must keep going.'

We got as far as Samara, as stowaways on a passenger ship and there we got jobs on a barge. After seven days we had reached the shores of the Caspian almost without incident, and there we found work with a small guild of fishermen in the filthy Kalmyk fishery of Kabankul-bai.

MORE ABOUT PENGUINS
AND PELICANS

Penguinews, which appears every month, contains details of all the new books issued by Penguins as they are published. From time to time it is supplemented by our stocklist, which includes around 5,000 titles.

A specimen copy of *Penguinews* will be sent to you free on request. Please write to Dept EP, Penguin Books Ltd, Harmondsworth, Middlesex, for your copy.

In the U.S.A.: For a complete list of books available from Penguins in the United States write to Dept CS, Penguin Books, 625 Madison Avenue, New York, New York 10022.

In Canada: For a complete list of books available from Penguins in Canada write to Penguin Books Canada Ltd, 2801 John Street, Markham, Ontario L3R 1B4.

PENGUIN CLASSICS

Some translations from the Russian

MAXIM GORKY
MY CHILDHOOD
Translated by Ronald Wilks

MAXIM GORKY
MY APPRENTICESHIP
Translated by Ronald Wilks

ANTON CHEKHOV
LADY WITH LAPDOG AND OTHER STORIES
Translated by David Magarshack

FYODOR DOSTOYEVSKY
THE BROTHERS KARAMAZOV Volumes 1 and 2
Translated by David Magarshack

NIKOLAI GOGOL
DEAD SOULS
Translated by David Magarshack

MIKHAIL LERMONTOV
A HERO OF OUR TIME
Translated by Paul Foote

ALEXANDER PUSHKIN
THE QUEEN OF SPADES AND OTHER STORIES
Translated by Rosemary Edmonds

LEO TOLSTOY
WAR AND PEACE Volumes 1 and 2
Translated by Rosemary Edmonds